FOREWORD FRAUD

A SHELF INDULGENCE COZY MYSTERY

S.E. BABIN

To another weird year, my friends, and the good books that sustain us. Cheers!

ONE

The town of Silverwood Hollow exploded into color during the fall months. Orange, red, and brilliant yellow leaved trees lined the main strip of road in the town, causing tourists to slow down and gawk. Traffic from October through December tended to be headache inducing at minimum and a nightmare at worst. I whipped my old Rav 4 into the parking spot right in front of Tattered Pages after sitting in traffic three times longer than normal and grumbled as I killed the engine.

I loved this time of year as the tourists brought in a lot of business, but getting to my beloved bookstore took me twice as long as normal. I sat in the car for a minute, listening to the ticking of the cooling engine. Poppy, my grumpy long haired Persian cat, sat in the store's window display staring at me balefully. Sometimes I could take her home, but sometimes she flat out refused to get in her carrier. At first, I'd been horrified when the former owner told me if I wanted the bookstore, I had to take the cat. Then I'd been even more horrified when he told me the cat never left the store. For a horrifying moment, I'd wondered if he sold me a ghost cat because I rarely saw her the first month or so I'd been there.

I worked for a while to get Poppy to come home with me once she finally deigned to show her face, but the cat had refused to get in her carrier. Eventually I realized Poppy hated the carrier, so now I had a little hammock installed in the second row of seats so she could hop in there and lounge on the way home.

If you'd told me a couple of years ago I'd be catering to a cat, I would have laughed in your face. Now Poppy has special food, a cat hammock, and the run of my bookstore whenever she wanted. Just then, once I locked eyes with her, the cat turned and fluffed her tail up as she hopped down and took off between the stacks.

I rolled my eyes and grabbed the coffee I'd bought at Spilling the Tea, a new shop close to my house. They served more tea than coffee, but the coffee they made was to die for.

Juggling my keys and purse, I unlocked the doors to the shop and stepped inside.

Kicking the door shut behind me, I dumped everything on the counter and turned the lock to make sure customers didn't come in early. Harper, my assistant, had been off for several days so I had extra steps to take before I could open. I'd never taken her for granted, but being here by myself for over a week let me know I needed to give Harper a pay raise. She took a lot of the burden from me, and I hadn't quite realized it until she was gone.

I called for Poppy, but she ignored me. I snorted. Par for the course with that cat, but I knew she'd zoom over once I filled her bowl. Humming to myself, I flipped the lights on to the store and smiled as they buzzed to life. The store lit up around me, the familiar smell and look of the tall bookshelves warming a place deep inside of me.

Not too long ago, I'd been involved in a murder investigation after I stumbled over the body of a customer. It had shaken me to the core, and I wondered if Silverwood Hollow was the right place for me for a while afterward. Those fears lifted as soon as I stepped back into Tattered Pages for the first time since the criminal was captured. This was my home. My shop. And I hoped to be here for a really long time.

THE BELL over the door jangled less than a minute after I flipped the sign to *Open*. I didn't recognize the first person who walked in, but that wasn't uncommon, especially during this time of year.

"Welcome to Tattered Pages!" I called out.

The woman smiled at me and wandered off to the romance section. We'd just gotten in a new steamy bestseller, and I noticed her gaze wander over to it. I smiled to myself and went back to my list of new books I needed to order. I ordered mostly from the bestseller lists for the tourists. For the regulars, I sent out an email survey a few times a year asking what people wanted. Usually it was a mix of mystery, romance, epic fantasy, and thrillers, but this year we had several teens take an interest in reading after the library started a Young Adult book club. I wanted people to read no matter how they found their books - legally, that is, but I'd noticed more and more young people coming over to Tattered Pages and browsing my selection.

I tucked the Sarah J. Maas Throne of Glass books on the front of the YA display, except for her romance series. I put those into the adult section. The last thing I needed in a small town like this was an angry parent lecturing me on the content of the book their teenager picked up. I tried to read almost every book I purchased, but it was impossible to read them all. Not that I didn't want to. There was never enough time in my life to read everything I wanted.

I left the woman to browse and went back to choosing books for my next large order. There were some rare ones I wanted to purchase, but I had to research pricing first to make sure I wasn't overpaying. Later today, I had a ticket to a lecture on rare books given in the next town over in Candlelight Springs. I enjoyed going there, but the town was full of odd people, and I tended to do whatever business I had and hightail it out of there. Strange things happened in Candlelight Springs.

I preferred Silverwood Hollow's special brand of quirky rather than Candlelight's potential of things that went bump in the night.

The woman browsed for a few more minutes and came to the register with a stack full of paranormal romance. I smiled at her and rang everything up.

"Visiting?" I inquired.

She shook her head. "I'm new to town." Her lips pressed together, and she looked down. "My divorce was finalized yesterday, and I thought I'd get a new start."

I gasped in surprise. My hand flew to my heart as my cheeks reddened with embarrassment. "I am so sorry. I didn't mean to pry." The woman was young, mid-twenties, if I had to guess. Her face was heart-shaped, and her eyes were a dark and stormy gray. She wore little makeup, and her face was pretty but drawn in sadness. She wore her auburn hair in a high, loose bun, and tendrils of soft curls fell around her face.

She offered a sad smile. "It's okay. Really. Yesterday was a tough day." She held up a Nalini Singh book. "That's why

I'm here. Love stories in the books are always better than the ones in real life, aren't they?"

I wouldn't know. My love life was DOA and had been for years. Dating in a small town wasn't for the faint of heart, and I'd done a lot less dating than most of the single people around here. First, I found dates awkward and full of falsehood. You had to dress up better than you normally do 95% of the time. You skimmed over personal details and yet offered extremely personal details like how many kids you wanted or if you'd ever been in prison. You had to decide how far or how cautious you needed to be, whether you'd have one, two, or heaven forbid three glasses of wine.

I found the entire thing exhausting. Recently, I'd flirted a little with a handsome detective, but I hadn't seen him in quite a while. Not much happened in a town like this, so there was no real reason for me to be involved with the local authorities. While that was a relief, I found I missed talking to him. Not enough to call him, though. The Silverwood Hollow gossip chain was a very real and terrifying thing to behold. Part of me, the one with more than a healthy dose of paranoia, wondered if my line was tapped and the second I picked up the phone to call him was the second the little old ladies in this town would start planning my wedding.

Then there was Cole. We started off rocky but ended up forming a wonderful friendship. Sometimes I thought his glances were a little more than friendly, but he'd been nothing but the perfect gentleman. Either way, I was glad to have friends in this town. I'd pushed dating to the back burner of my life long ago and was content to leave it that way.

"I'm Dakota," I said instead of answering her question. I offered my hand to shake, and she took it as she offered a tentative smile.

"Lauren. I bought a house on Eastwood Street."

My eyes widened. "The old Chambers' house?" It was the only one available in that area, but the house was a remodeling nightmare. The roof was almost caved in on one side and it listed just slightly to the right, hinting at serious foundation problems.

She nodded and laughed at the look on my face. "My husband," she began and winced. "*Ex*-husband worked in banking. I have a cushion."

I didn't pry. "Good luck. That house is the talk of the Silverwood Hollow gazette at least once a week."

"Mrs. Randall?" she asked, and we locked eyes and laughed.

So, the old busybody struck again. Mrs. Randall was a bit of a legend around this town. If it happened, she knew it. If it hadn't happened, she probably knew it too. The Campbell house made her irrationally angry and once a week, she sent a letter to the local newspaper complaining about the state of the house. I stopped reading the local paper, so I hadn't known the house sold.

"She put a timeline on the remodel of the house and asked for construction to begin after 9 a.m. and stop by 5 p.m." Lauren rolled her eyes.

A snort escaped me. "Well, I can't wait to see what you do with the house. It's been an eyesore for years around here."

The Chambers' house had a bit of a sordid historical history, and it was the reason the house took so long to sell. Historical homes couldn't be remodeled without the permission of the city and a lot of people didn't want the hassle, so they never made an offer. However, the entire city was annoyed with the state of disrepair, and they were champing at the bit to get the house sold and repaired.

"The remodel starts next week. It took me a while to get the paperwork and figure out exactly what I wanted to do. Then it took forever for me to find someone willing to do the kind of work I wanted. I want to preserve everything I can, but I do want some modern touches."

I finished ringing Lauren up and handed the books over to her. "There's a great bakery just a door or two down. If you're up for it, how about we grab a cup of coffee and a muffin later this week?"

Her face lit up. "I'd love that." She took her bag. "Thanks so much for the warm welcome, Dakota."

I shrugged. "I'm befriending you only so I can keep up with the house remodel," I joked, but grinned at her to make sure she understood I was only kidding.

"If that's the case, I'm going to have a town full of friends soon!" Lauren waved at me and left the store, the bell over the door jingling merrily in her absence.

THE STORE STAYED busy for the majority of the day, most of them tourists wandering in from their exploration of the other shops in the town square. I had to stop one person from coming in with a huge coffee topped with a mountain of whipped cream. Normally I didn't mind when someone came in with coffee, but that one had an open lid and looked ready to explode at any given moment. Maybe a lost sale. Maybe not. Better than damaging some of the expensive merchandise in the store, though.

At 2 p.m. I flipped the sign to *Closed* and gathered up my belongings. Candlelight Springs took about 15 minutes to get to if the traffic was light. I checked Poppy's bowl to make sure she'd eaten and called out a goodbye to her as I locked the store up. The cat didn't bother to respond, but she'd eaten, so I knew she was okay.

I caught some light traffic on the way into the other town, but I'd given myself a cushion of time just in case. The lecture was at Binders, a competing bookstore owned by a woman named Harriet Tulle. I'd met her in a restaurant when I was investigating the murder of a woman who'd purchased a book from me. We hadn't spoken since then, but I looked forward to seeing her again.

I pulled into the parking lot of Binders, impressed with the number of customers she had today. The shop was a standalone structure and had a cute, scalloped awning with the store's name done in a fancy script font. As I got closer, I peeked in at the window display. Jealousy clawed its way up my spine, even though I tried my best to suppress it. I needed to up my display game, apparently.

She had the newest paranormal cozy mystery from one of the New York publishers set up in a display that would make any baker jealous. The book focused on a wedding planner who spoke to ghosts. Harriet had set up what I hoped was a fake three-tier wedding cake along with a pile of elegantly wrapped wedding gifts, all done in a tasteful cream and salmon color. The book was set on top of the wedding cake along with a banner proclaiming the new release and a scheduled author signing in the next two weeks.

She'd managed to get Jenna Bateman to sign here? My lips turned down in a frown but knew my lack of authors was my own fault. Networking had always been difficult for me, but I knew my shop needed to get with the times. I tore my gaze away from the gorgeous display and went inside the store.

Harriet stood at the register, ringing a line of customers up. The shop was larger than mine and decorated in tasteful creams and sage greens. A prominent display of new releases met customers the moment they walked in and there was even a quirky sign pointing them to the sections they needed to browse. To the left of it stood another sign telling me the rare books lecture was straight ahead.

I waved at Harriet as I walked to the lecture area. Her eyes widened with surprise, and she gave me a wide grin. She held up a finger telling me to wait, so I browsed the best-sellers section while she finished up. The lecture didn't start for another twenty minutes, so I had a little time. I wanted a good seat, though, so I couldn't wait for too long.

Harriet made her way over to me just a couple of minutes later. She was a shorter woman with shoulder length dark hair curled tastefully around her friendly face. Her brown eyes crinkled at the edges as she rushed over to greet me.

"Dakota! What a surprise. I can only assume you're here for the lecture?"

I nodded. "I've been meaning to add in some additional rare books and wanted to get more professional feedback. I've followed Lindsay MacIntosh's work for a while."

Harriet nodded thoughtfully. "I don't do a lot of work in rare books, but I have people asking for them all the time.

Lindsay's work popped up in one of the trade journals I subscribe to, so I reached out and asked if she'd be interested in doing a talk here."

I nodded. "Good on you. I'm a terrible networker," I confessed. "I have to get better about reaching out to artists and authors to bring them into the store."

Harriet gave me a long look. "You really should, Dakota. Your shop is right on the water and in the heart of town. It's perfect to draw tourists in. There's a wonderful opportunity to bring in more business, especially with people vacationing and looking for things to do."

Harriet was right, but I still bristled at the lecturing tone. "I'll get it," I said, trying to keep the coolness I felt out of my tone. "It's still a work in progress."

Harriet patted me on the shoulder, her gaze seeing too much. "There's enough for everyone, darling. We have to stick together, you know. Bookstores are becoming a dying breed and we both know how desperately we need them."

Guilt flooded me, and I nodded, ashamed of the jealousy and irritation I felt. "Well, I'm here to learn. That's the first step."

We smiled at each other; the tension forgotten. She walked me over to the back of the store where several rows of chairs were set up. At the front sat a table covered with a black tablecloth and a colorful logo that read *Macintosh's*

Rare & Vintage Books, and an address in Maine printed on the bottom.

Lindsay stood at the front, her tastefully styled hair pulled into an elegant chignon. She wore a suit that would look better in the boardroom instead of a casual bookstore and heels that had to be killing her toes. She smiled at me, but it didn't reach her eyes. Her gaze gave me a quick once over from head to toe, and from the way she dismissed me, I thought maybe she didn't like what she saw.

I looked down at my striped comfortable canvas shoes and my skinny jeans and inwardly shrugged. I hadn't come here to impress anyone.

A few people had already taken up most of the front row. I chose a seat at the end of the second row, the last one slightly angled so no one's head got in the way. Once I sat, I pulled out a notebook and a pen from my purse and waited for things to start. Harriet walked over to Lindsay and asked her if she needed anything to drink.

The woman sniffed and asked for a mimosa. I pressed my lips together to keep from laughing at Harriet's dumbstruck expression.

"I have coffee, herbal tea, and water," Harriet said after a moment. "We don't have the proper licensing to serve alcohol."

Lindsay huffed an annoyed breath. "A bottle of Perrier then."

Harriet stood there for a moment and eventually turned without saying a word. The odds of her having Perrier were low. Lindsay might just have to be parched or resign herself to drinking good ol' regular bottled water.

A few minutes later, more of the chairs began to fill up. There was still about ten minutes left before the lecture began. I didn't think she'd have a full house, regardless of the time the lecture started. Rare books were a niche thing no matter where you were, and a town in the mountains of Virginia probably wouldn't bring a big draw.

I found it strange that Lindsay would say yes to coming all the way out here for a lecture, but it benefited me, so I wasn't questioning anything.

A few minutes later, Harriet came over with a regular bottle of water and handed it to Lindsay, who looked down at it like it was a rattlesnake. Without a word, Harriet set it on the table and walked away.

I swallowed down a smile.

At 3.p.m. on the dot, Lindsay began the lecture. I didn't know what to expect, but a PowerPoint and music wasn't it. The speakers boomed with a tinny sound as action movie music sounded from them. I peeked over at Harriet, who stood by one of the shelves with an expression that told me she thought Lindsay MacIntosh had lost her mind.

"Good afternoon!" Lindsay's voice boomed through the store. Harriet winced at the sound. Bookstores weren't libraries, but there was still an unwritten noise rule in place. Lindsay trampled all over that and then set it on fire.

As she spoke, I settled into my seat, the notebook forgotten beside me. Lindsay reminded me of one of those big-time corporate people who used huge words like "strategic" and "imminent" without them meaning anything at all. It was twenty minutes in when I went from bored to suspicious.

"If you're interested in having a partner in your rare and vintage book sourcing efforts, I'm offering a package right now at 25% off." Her eyes were bright with a sales fervor. I looked around at the people sitting around me and saw a variety of expressions. Some yawned behind their hands, some looked at Lindsay with something akin to hero worship, but the vast majority, including Harriet, now studied her with suspicion.

"We form a partnership; that's exactly what this will be—a true partnership—and you tell me the books you're looking for and I'll source them at a huge discount. I then pass those savings on to you ..."

I sighed and stood up, gathering my belongings. Just as I was about to step out of the aisle, several other people stood up and gathered their things, too. My gaze locked with Lindsay's, and the hostility beaming from them stopped me dead in my tracks. I glanced over at Harriet, who suddenly straightened and headed directly over to Lindsay.

I cringed and hurried out of the store. I'd learned absolutely nothing today and felt cheated I'd wasted my time on what was an obvious sales pitch. Next time I'd do further digging before signing up for something like this.

I looked back and saw Harriet engaged in deep discussion with Lindsay. Both looked angry.

I felt glad I wasn't in Harriet's shoes today.

TWO

I'd just opened my car door and was about to get in when I saw a familiar blond head bobbing through the parking lot. I shut the door and jogged over to chat with Cole.

His green eyes lit up when he saw me. "Dakota!"

I pulled my purse up higher on my shoulder. "What brings you out here?" Cole and I had a good relationship, but we carefully toed the line between his job and my curiosity. The first time we met, he grilled me about my involvement in Marcy's murder investigation, and I didn't trust him. We had a spoken and unspoken agreement now never to mix work with our friendship.

Cole looked down, but not before I saw an emotion I couldn't identify flash in his eyes. "Just covering the lecture today." He held up the camera slung around his neck and gave me a sheepish, slightly guilty smile.

Hmm. Cole was lying to me about something. One of my eyebrows went up. "Things aren't going so well in there, so you might be able to catch a scoop if you hurry up."

His eyes widened, and he looked toward the entrance.

I snorted and held my hands up. "I won't keep you."

He fidgeted before he squeezed my arm. "Thanks, Dakota! I won't forget this!" Cole took off at a run, his lean body slicing through the wind as he made his way inside.

Shaking my head, I got back into my Rav 4 and headed back to Silverwood Hollow.

BACK AT TATTERED PAGES, I'd just finished up dusting all the shelves when my cell phone rang. I'd been back for several hours and decided to tidy up the shop since I'd left the lecture early. This was on my to-do list and had been for ages, but I continually pushed it off because I always found some way to procrastinate on it. Today, with a closed shop and nothing else on my schedule, I realized if I put it off again, I might have to do a self-procrastination intervention.

Grateful for the break, I hit the green button without looking to see who it was. "Dakota," I chirped.

I knew the voice on the line like I knew the back of my hand. "Miss Adair, this is Detective Cavanaugh."

Uh oh. We'd reverted from first names to titles. This couldn't be good. I decided to push his buttons a little. "Hello, Hardy. Long time no hear."

He went silent on the phone, as if my words surprised him. He chuckled over the line. "Sorry, Dakota. This is official business."

"How can I help you?" I put down the duster and leaned against one of the shelves, my phone tucked between my ear and shoulder. His voice slid like silk over my skin, deep and dark.

Not good, Dakota. Get your head out of the clouds. I couldn't count the number of women wandering through Tattered Pages on any given day talking about the new handsome detective and wondering about his marital status. Crime had never been a problem in this town until recently, but we still didn't have much to write home about. Either there was a crime spike in this town or word traveled like wildfire around here. I suspected the latter.

"Harriet Tulle mentioned you were at Binders today."

I straightened. "I was."

"Did you see Lindsay Macintosh?"

"I did. I signed up for her talk on rare books."

He made a noncommittal sound. "And how long did you stay?"

I thought back. The original lecture was supposed to go for two hours. "An hour maybe?"

"You left early?" I could hear the scratch of his pen on paper through the line.

"I did."

"Why is that?"

A sigh escaped me. "Is this an interrogation, Hardy?"

The pen paused. "No, merely establishing a timeline."

"Is everything okay?"

Silence fell over the line. I could practically see the wheels spinning in his brain. "Normally I wouldn't divulge this information," he said, "but we all know how fast the Silverwood Hollow gossip chain is."

I couldn't help it. I laughed out loud. "Especially when crime or romance are the subject."

A horrible thought struck me. "Cole. Is he okay?" My heart fluttered like a rabbit in my chest.

"Cole was there?" A disapproving note sounded in his tone. He and Cole hadn't gotten off to the best start, either, but they never managed to straighten out their relationship. I guessed they never would. It would be difficult for a detective to have a friendship with a reporter constantly on the hunt for a scoop.

"I ran into him in the parking lot."

"Did he say why he was there?"

Cole's odd behavior surfaced in my mind. "He said he was covering the lecture. I told him to hurry up and get in there before he missed his scoop."

"You never answered why you left early," Hardy said, diverting the subject back to Lindsay.

"It ended up being a sales pitch and not a learning opportunity." Annoyance filled me. Even though I'd left and didn't get tangled up with Lindsay's company, the wasted time still ate at me. I wasn't someone who lived or died by a schedule, but I liked having my day planned out. I thought for sure I'd come back to Tattered Pages with a good plan in hand. The thought of expanding the store had been in my mind more and more these days, but I couldn't do that without bolstering my business.

"What kind of sales opportunity?"

I told Hardy what I remembered, which wasn't much. I'd left before I got to the meat and bones of it.

"Hmm. Back to Cole. Did he seem preoccupied? Anything out of the ordinary?"

It felt like a betrayal to Hardy, but I wasn't going to tell him that I thought Cole was lying to me. "Not really. He just seemed like he was on the hunt for a good story. Cole always gets a little preoccupied when he can smell a scoop."

"Anything else you can remember?"

I told him about Harriet and Lindsay's conversation once I left and the small row over the drinks. "I don't think that's important, but you never know what it might mean."

The pen stopped, and I heard it drop onto something with a thump. Hardy sighed and let out a slow breath. "This is helpful, Dakota. I really appreciate it."

"Any time." Before I could regret it, I spoke again. "Don't be a stranger, Hardy. I haven't seen you in ages."

"I've been wanting to get over to Sprinkle Heaven and try Trudy's new spiced hot chocolate, but I've been swamped with work. For a place with no crime rate, this town sure has been busy since I got here."

A wide grin spread over my face. "Curious," I mused. "They must be testing you out, making sure you're equipped for the job."

"I doubt it's that," he grumbled. "You won't believe how many cats have been treed over the last two weeks. A few weeks before that, we had a rash of peeping Tom complaints."

The grin on my face spread. "That must be tiring," I said, my voice sweet as sugar.

"You're making fun of me," he said with mock outrage.

"Well, you're the first young and single man this town has seen in ages. I'm not surprised about the 'spike' in crime. And let me guess, they're asking for you by name?"

You could have heard a pin drop over the line. Hardy muttered something unflattering. "I wondered why all of a sudden I was getting called out to these ridiculous things!"

"Welcome to Silverwood Hollow, Hardy Cavanaugh. You're the hottest thing since Mrs. Rafferty set her husband's shed on fire."

"Goodbye, Dakota," Hardy growled.

"Bye now, Most Eligible Bachelor."

I hung up before he could say anything else, only to remember he hadn't told me what was going on.

Darn. Maybe I'd stop by Trudy's shop to see if she'd heard anything.

And maybe I'd buy myself a cupcake too.

THREE

If there was a heaven on Earth, it had to be Trudy's *Sprinkle Heaven*. The proprietor was an older woman, her dyed red hair seeing the first sprinklings of silver. I knew she wouldn't have those for long. Trudy was fastidious about keeping up the appearance of her scarlet hair and her extreme false eyelashes. That being said, she was one of the friendliest people I knew, and she made the best muffins on this side of the east coast.

"Hey Dakota!" Trudy said from behind the display case. She pointed over to the adorably decorated chalkboard. "Check out the specials today. I think you're going to like them."

I'm not sure why she told me that. Trudy knew I liked just about everything she made. Just recently she'd come up with an insane coffee drink for the Harvest Festival. I hadn't heard much about it since she'd won first place, but I was dying to see it come onto the menu.

I'd asked about it once and she said she was having a hard time sourcing all the ingredients, but she hadn't mentioned it since. I looked over on the board and saw the spiced hot chocolate she normally had this time of year, but she'd also added snickerdoodle cookies and a seven-layer Christmas brownie. My eyebrows went up at that one.

"Seven layers?" I inquired. "Do tell."

Trudy's smile beamed. "Chocolate, salted caramel, a cheese-cake filling, a layer of Dulce de Leche, a cinnamon chocolate syrup drizzle, a layer of crushed Heath bars, and topped off with homemade salted caramel and white chocolate chips."

I gaped at her.

"That's exactly the kind of look I want to see when I tell people what's in it," she said as she held up her tongs and clicked them. "Want to try one?"

I did, but my hips didn't. However, anything in Trudy's shop was difficult to resist. "Can you cut one in half for me? I'll take the other half to go."

Trudy gave me a knowing smile and took a brownie out of the case. She expertly cut it with a serrated knife and tucked the other half of it into a paper box. "Coffee?" she asked as she handed the plate over the top of the case.

"Always." I rummaged through my purse and pulled out a ten. She rang me up with the customary 25% discount I always objected to and handed me back my change.

"Coffee preference?" she asked.

"Anything new today?"

"I have the spiced hot chocolate, but if you're feeling lucky, I'll whip you up something freestyle."

Trudy's freestyle coffees were brilliant. "Absolutely," I said as I tucked the change back into my purse. I took my brownie and headed over to one of the tables tucked into a back corner. The shop itself was a cute little mainstay a few doors down from mine. Olive Twist– a specialty oil shop– was close as well. Jen, the proprietor, also was brilliant when it came to different oil blends and the bread pairings with it. Ever since I'd bought my shop, I had to be careful with my weight because everything those ladies had was delicious.

I waited for Trudy to come over with the coffee. She always sat and chatted with me for at least five minutes if the shop was slow, and I'd made sure to come at a time when she wouldn't be bombarded with people.

Sure enough, she headed over with a steaming cup, a mountain of whipped cream on the top. When she sat down and pushed it over to me, the scent of cardamom and cinnamon wafted up. The tension of the day fell away from my shoulders. I inhaled deeply.

"What is this?"

She shrugged. "I don't come up with names. Just concepts. That's a mix of hot chocolate and espresso combined with a pump of Dulce de Leche syrup and a sprinkle of cardamom and cinnamon."

I took a sip and closed my eyes in bliss. "You have to keep this. It has all the good things chocolate has and all the good things coffee has. It's like a chocolatey, spicy, holiday drink."

Trudy beamed at me. "I'll write it down as soon as I get back to the register," she said. "So, you never come in here at this time unless you want to chat about something. What's on your mind?"

Busted. Trudy was shrewder than I'd given her credit for. "Have you heard anything come through the grapevine yet?"

One of her reddish eyebrows went up. "The Silverwood Silverettes?"

I snorted. This was the unofficial name of the Silverwood gossip line. "That's the one. I got a call from Detective Cavanaugh. He's asking a lot of questions about a lecturer who came to speak at Binders."

Trudy's nose wrinkled. "You went to Binders? You're slumming with the competition now?"

Trudy was well aware of my thoughts on competing bookstores, but as I recalled Harriet's patient and kind tone, guilt filled me. "Yes, well, maybe I was wrong about that store," I confessed. "Harriet had a rare book lecturer come out for a talk today."

"I'm assuming by the look on your face it didn't go so well."

I shook my head. "I left early. Harriet didn't seem pleased either once it took a turn for the salesy."

Her eyes narrowed. "How can you be salesy in a lecture like that?"

"She wanted to partner up with bookstores in the area. Something like a finder's fee, I guess."

Trudy harrumphed. "Sounds like you could do a better job in your sleep," she said.

I didn't disagree. A lot of my research came from scouring industry boards, eBay, and other sites where people were selling their books. A little came from the actual rare book dealers, though I found sometimes the market didn't always agree with their opinions. Sometimes I scoured estate sales and found amazing deals on private collections. Those were always the best for me. I'd made enough money to pay my mortgage several times over with the private collections books I'd found. And, I tended to keep more of the ones I purchased that way because they were less expensive than buying them outright from a dealer or auction site.

"I'm not opposed to eventually bringing in a partner," I admitted, "but I don't want to pay someone to do just that for me. I don't need any help in that area. I need someone more on the publicity side. I'm not the best at networking or reaching outside of the town to bring in talent for author signings. It's just not comfortable for me."

Trudy smiled at me. "I'll check the Silverwood Silverette pipeline to see what comes back. No idea what it could be?" she questioned as she stood.

I shook my head. "Probably something about Lindsay MacIntosh. I don't know the specifics, but he asked a lot of questions about her."

"I'll find out what I can and let you know if I hear anything." She waved her fingers at me and went back behind the display.

I sat at Trudy's for quite a while enjoying the snack she'd dished up for me, not worrying one bit whether I'd ruin my dinner.

I was the only one cooking so it might be a salad night.

POPPY WANTED to come home with me that evening and she easily hopped into the cat hammock as soon as I deposited her in the passenger seat. She yowled at me when she thought I took too long to start the car, especially since the air was frigid and rapidly cooling. Snow was scheduled for next week and while a part of me wasn't looking forward to the change in temps, the other part of me was excited because it meant we were one step closer to a white Christmas.

However, I'd become woefully behind on my holiday shopping. Again, this was part of the procrastination habits I'd been trying to break. I didn't have a lot of people to shop for. Just my mom and a few friends. I usually gifted Harper an extra day off and tried to find her a new book she'd never read before. Easier said than done. Harper read just about as much as I did.

This year, I'd managed to find her a rare copy of *Little Women*, a book I'd been astounded to find out she'd never read. I'd gotten it for a steal on eBay when someone didn't realize exactly what they had, and it had just arrived a few days ago. I'd tucked it into my nightstand so I wouldn't misplace it, but as I eyed the almost pristine cover, I longed to have it and get Harper something else.

This happened to me every single year. If it was a book, especially a classic, I coveted it.

I opened the fridge out of habit, not hungry exactly but knowing if I didn't at least eat a little something, I'd wake up in the middle of the night starving.

Yesterday's leftovers hung out at the right of the fridge - a pasta dish I'd made from a sketchy website that I immediately regretted. There'd been more than a few of those over the last few months. Cooking for one wasn't an easy business.

Then there was the salad stuff I tended to skip over especially if I could fit Italian into the menu. I had a few tv dinners in the freezer, but I tried to stay away from those just on principle. I'm not sure why considering I'd demolished half of a seven-layer brownie a mere hour or so ago.

I settled on a chicken breast dish with pesto sauce, though I regretfully left off the pasta this time. I added a touch of cream into the pesto to make it easy to spread and I roasted a couple of cups of broccoli in the oven. My vegetable intake left something to be desired, but I was trying to get better about that too.

While the chicken and broccoli cooked, I scrolled through all the text messages I'd missed today.

Mom sent me a message about half an hour ago complaining about the new fridge she'd bought and how it had broken right when she'd just gotten back from grocery shopping. I fired off a text to her asking if she'd found someone to repair it yet.

Mom responded right back.

Yes, a handsome single man your age.

I rolled my eyes.

Good, I typed back. I *wish you the best in your new relationship.*

Dakota! Mom sent back. *You should be ashamed of yourself.*

I'm not interested.

Mom was hinting around about grandbabies more than usual, much to my consternation. Babies weren't on the horizon and hadn't been for years. It hadn't stopped her from asking, though. Not directly. That wasn't her style. It was more, "Ooh, Dakota, just look at that precious little outfit," in the mall, or "That Cole fellow. Is he single? I'm sure he'd make a nice boyfriend." I rolled my eyes each and every time she said something like that and tried not to take offense.

Mom and Dad didn't have any other children so there were no siblings she could pester. When we lost Dad seven years ago to cancer, Mom spiraled with grief, and it took her a long time to come out of it. I know she saw the potential loss of his bloodline. I didn't think about things that way, but I knew Mom still grieved him every day.

Recently, she'd made mention of getting back into the dating pool again. I thought it would be a wonderful thing for her, but the thought of it made my heart hurt. There was only one Bob. No one would ever be able to replace my dad. But I didn't want Mom to be lonely and so she had my full blessing. Whenever she was ready to date again, I'd support her.

No babies on the horizon, Mom. Just me and my lonely dinners.

Mom didn't take the bait on that one.

I love you, honey, she texted. *Let's have dinner soon and catch up.*

Mom was just down the road. We didn't need a reason to catch up, but we did need to start up our weekly dinners again. Things had been so hectic, I hadn't had the opportunity to break away from things to cook something for her.

We still saw each other, but it was usually in passing. Recently, Mom had taken up yoga, even though she complained about the new French teacher. Even though she didn't like her, she continued to go to class which made me think maybe Mom had a bit of the green-eyed monster especially since the woman was Mom's age.

Love you too, I typed back just as the oven timer went off.

Poppy came shooting around the corner, knowing when the timer went off something was cooking. I slipped on a potholder and took the broccoli out of the oven. When she smelled it, she yowled loudly. If a cat could be annoyed, Poppy's expression nailed it. The cat couldn't roll her eyes, but I felt the judgment oozing from her as she turned tail and walked away.

"Go ahead, cat. You have no idea I have delicious chicken on the stovetop."

Poppy walked away, her backend sashaying and her tail up in the air on her way out of the kitchen.

I DISHED up my food and plopped myself down in front of the television. I tried my best to break that bad habit but eating at the kitchen table made my lonely house even more pronounced, so now I usually ate in front of the t.v. idly flipping through Netflix.

As soon as I finished the last bite of chicken, the phone rang.

"Dakota!" Trudy's trembling voice came over the line. "It's me. You're never going to believe what happened!"

I set my fork down and sat up. "Please don't tell me it was a murder," I said just as Trudy blurted, "There's been another murder!

FOUR

Lindsay MacIntosh had been found dead in her car right outside of Binders. The driver's side door was left open and the only reason someone checked was because of the incessant dinging. She'd left her keys in the car just as someone had come up to her and bludgeoned her over the head with something heavy.

At least that's what Trudy told me, her words coming breathless and excited as she relayed all the gossip over the line.

"That's two murders in just a little while," I murmured.

"This one is in Candlelight Springs, though," Trudy said.

A laugh escaped me. "Which is less than fifteen minutes away," I reminded her. "This town has some bad juju going on with it. Or something."

Trudy sighed. "Honey, every fifteen years or so this town goes through something. Usually it isn't murder, but we have our fair share of divorces, property crimes, burglaries, and vandalism."

"I know." Trudy was right. Crime wasn't all that common, but sometimes we'd have things pop up one after the other. Some residents blamed the moon, even if the crimes didn't happen on the full moon. Some people blamed the teenagers and their parents for letting them run roughshod over the neighborhood (their words), and others saw it as a sign of the end times. I thought things came in stages. It's how it had always been, but murders were extremely uncommon and now we'd had two in a short time period.

"That's a real shame," I said mostly to myself. "Do they have any idea who did it?"

"Now that's real interesting, Dakota," Trudy said as if she was waiting on me to ask her the exact same thing. "There are three witnesses who said she and Cole Gardener were fighting right before she died!"

I gasped out loud. I'd known Cole had been there, but he was no murderer. What he wanted with her probably had nothing to do with the lecture, if I had to guess based on his behavior, but he hadn't divulged anything else. "Is he in jail?"

"Heavens no," she said. "The Silverettes said everything

looks circumstantial right now." I had to laugh. God bless the little old ladies who watched too much *Law and Order*.

"Circumstantial, huh?" I mused. "Maybe I should call Cole."

"I wouldn't," Trudy warned. "Word is he's been in a bad mood all week."

And wasn't that curious? I made a mental note to check on him tomorrow. Whatever Cole was hiding wouldn't last long with the Silverettes around. Perhaps I could find out what it was first.

And hope it didn't have anything to do with the murder of Lindsay MacIntosh.

Cole wasn't a killer, but Detective Cavanaugh wouldn't care too much about that if he focused on Cole as the suspect. He didn't know the man like I did. Cole Gardener was a sweet, wonderful person and whatever Lindsay had done to him, he wouldn't react in a way that would harm her. She didn't seem like the best kind of person, but I tried not to judge. Maybe she was having a bad day. Maybe things weren't working out in her career like she wanted them to. Based upon that ridiculous sales pitch earlier, maybe I'd hit the nail on the head. Seems like maybe she needed money and was desperate to take on new partnerships.

But the whole thing seemed sleazy, and I didn't want anything to do with it. Thus the reason I walked out once she'd gone from lecturer to salesman. No one deserved to die, though.

Trudy and I chatted for a little while longer. When we hung up, my fingers scrolled through my contact list until I pulled Cole up. I hesitated before I pressed his name, unsure if I should heed Trudy's warning or if he would like hearing from a friend. I set my phone down instead and rinsed off my dishes.

Moments later I was in the car heading over to Cole's house.

COLE LIVED in a small Craftsman style house about ten minutes away from mine. The lights were on, and his truck was parked in the driveway. The television screen sent flickers of light against the front window as I stood on the porch and knocked.

Cole opened the door and stared at me, surprise written on his face.

"Hi."

We said nothing for a moment. Cole normally looked well put together. Tonight, he looked like he'd been run ragged. A light five o'clock shadowed his jaw. His hair was unkempt and messy and instead of the well-tailored jeans and button downs he normally wore, Cole had on a pair of sweats and a loose t-shirt. I swallowed hard, unused to seeing him so vulnerable. He looked dangerously attractive tonight.

"I shouldn't have come," I said and turned to go.

"Dakota."

I stopped and waited.

Cole sighed. "Do you want to come in?"

I turned and peered at him. "I was going to call."

He nodded and held open the door. I followed him inside.

Cole and I hung out a lot together, but we'd never been to each other's houses. It was an almost unwritten rule. It seemed too intimate to me, and I liked the friendship we'd built even though it put some distance between us. However, it wasn't always easy for men and women to be friends, and this kept the rumor mill mostly silent. I'd heard a few rumors about us, but people seemed more confused than anything.

I liked to keep them off balance.

Cole's house was neat and clean, much like him. The interior smelled of lemon and lavender, a crisp smell I wasn't surprised by. The television was on the History Channel and a show about the Egyptian pyramids. Notes were scattered all over his coffee table, a scattering of Cole's handwriting and what looked like official documents.

"Do you want a glass of wine?" Cole went into the kitchen and poured out of an already open bottle.

I shook my head. "I just wanted to come by and see how you are."

His shoulders fell. "You heard about Lindsay."

It wasn't a question. I nodded.

"I had nothing to do with it."

"I know." I pulled out one of the barstools and sat down. "Want to tell me what happened?"

The sides of his mouth turned down in a frown. His eyes were full of regret. "Not really," he said.

I blinked in surprise. "Cole, the Silverettes said you were seen arguing with her before she died."

He squeezed his eyes shut. Cole's jaw went tense, and he flexed his fingers against the wineglass. "It doesn't mean I murdered her."

"I'm not saying you did. That's the opposite of what I'm saying. Detective Cavanaugh called me."

Cole's eyes snapped to me. "When?"

"Earlier today." I motioned for him to pour me a glass. "Small, please."

Cole pushed a glass over and I took a sip to steady my nerves.

"What did he want?" he asked.

"Normal things. Harriet told him I was there, and he wanted to know if I saw anything odd."

Cole stilled. "And did you?"

My gaze narrowed. "Did I what?"

He set his glass down. "See anything odd?"

My heartbeat picked up. "I'm not sure." I took another sip of my wine. "Tell me why you lied to me earlier."

Cole's lips pressed together. "I can't," he said after a moment. "It's for a story."

"Lindsay was part of it?"

He nodded. "Yes, I had the most reasons to keep her alive!"

"Cole, I–"

The doorbell rang just then. Cole stiffened and shut his eyes. "It's too late."

Fear filled me. "What's too late?" I asked. I reached for his arm.

"Cole Gardener! Open up."

My mouth dropped open. "Why is Cavanaugh here?"

His green eyes went dim. "To arrest me for murder."

FIVE

I stomped over to the front door and flung it open, meeting the stunned blue-eyed gaze of Hardy Cavanaugh. His surprise quickly fled and something else took its place. Something dark.

"Miss Adair," Hardy said, his voice frigid. "Is Mr. Gardener available?"

"Cut it out," I snapped. "Cole is my friend. Why are you here?"

Hardy's jaw went hard. "I'm not at liberty to discuss an active investigation with you."

I put my hands on my hips and glared at him. "Cole didn't kill her."

"And how do you know, Miss Adair? Were you there?" One of his eyebrows lifted. "Should I be looking somewhere else? Perhaps at you?" His tone was slow and laconic, but his eyes burned with anger.

"Come on, Hardy. You know I had nothing to do with it either."

"Perhaps you both had something to do with it. You two seem awfully cozy tonight. Is there something going on I should know about?"

"Nothing we're doing here is any of your business. If you're going to arrest him–"

Cole's hand touched my arm. "Dakota."

I tilted my head to look up at him. "You don't have to go."

Hardy snorted. "I beg to differ, Miss Adair."

"Is he under arrest?" I demanded.

Hardy and Cole stared each other down. "I'm here as a courtesy," Hardy finally said. "If you don't come down to the station with me tonight, officers will be here in the morning."

I glanced between the two men and saw some unspoken conversation happening until finally, Cole nodded. "Let me grab my jacket."

"Cole!"

He shook his head once. "It's going to happen either way.

At least now I can walk in with some dignity." Cole left us standing there, and I turned back to Hardy.

"You should be ashamed of yourself," I hissed.

Hardy sighed. "Dakota, he was the last one to see Lindsay. They got into an argument. My hands are tied on this and if you weren't emotionally involved, you'd see I'm right."

"Emotionally–" I choked off the rest of what I was going to say because it wouldn't have been productive either way. "Hardy, you know he isn't guilty."

His eyes shuttered. "I know what the evidence is telling me."

Cole walked back in just then, a jacket flung over one arm and a leather satchel in his other hand. He and Hardy nodded at each other.

"Lock up for me?" Cole asked.

I crossed my arms over my chest. "This is ridiculous."

"Dakota..." Cole pleaded. "Don't make this any harder than it needs to be."

"But you didn't kill that woman!" I protested.

Hardy stepped off the porch and walked down to his car. He hadn't taken a cruiser tonight, which was a blessing in disguise. If he had, the entire neighborhood would be on fire with gossip. As it was, even his presence would raise some eyebrows, but at least he didn't come in with guns blazing.

Cole watched until Hardy got into his car and leaned closer to me. His breath tickled my ear as he spoke. "I need you to investigate. Find out what Lindsay was hiding."

"I need you to tell me why you were arguing with her!"

He leaned back. "It doesn't matter."

"It does!"

But Cole shook his head and followed Hardy to the car.

"Cole!"

He stopped and turned, his green eyes pleading. "I need your help, but please accept I can't tell you everything."

Without waiting for me to respond, he turned and walked away.

I stood on the porch and watched Hardy's car until the taillights faded in the distance.

BACK AT HOME, I laid in bed wondering how in the world I was going to investigate a murder with exactly zero evidence. Well. Not zero, I suppose, but less than I had the first time I'd accidentally stumbled into a murder. I knew she and Cole had something going on - whether it was business or pleasure, I couldn't say. The tiny part of me that found Cole attractive squirmed at the thought of him being involved with Lindsay on a personal basis, but I had no right to protest. Cole and I were friends. That was all.

But wasn't it odd that Lindsay wound up dead almost immediately after having an argument with Cole? The timing was certainly suspicious. Could someone be after Cole? Could they have framed him? Or was this merely a crime of opportunity and someone saw the perfect moment to strike?

I groaned and rubbed my hands over my face. I didn't want to get involved in this, but I couldn't let Cole go down for something he didn't do. Then again, I didn't like the fact he wouldn't tell me what had happened between the two of them, because of what happened afterward.

Poppy hopped up on the dresser and stared at me balefully.

"What about you?" I asked the cat. "Got any tips?"

Poppy yowled and cleaned her paw. I sighed and flipped off the lamp light. Tomorrow I'd start trying to untangle this web. Tonight, I'd do my best to get some sleep.

Another murder mystery had dropped into my life way too soon.

SIX

The next morning dawn broke in rays of oranges and reds over the mountain tops. The air outside was crisp and cool, and I inhaled a deep breath before I stepped into Spilling the Tea. The proprietor of the shop was a woman named Lily, who was brand new to town. She had an almost ethereal look to her. Thin framed with a penchant for peasant skirts and floral patterns, Lily looked like a resident fairy, content to flit around pouring coffee for people and growing and mixing her own teas.

The scent of Bergamot and Lavender floated to me the second I stepped in.

"Hi Lily!" I called.

The woman looked up and waved when she saw me. "Same as usual?" she asked.

I almost said yes, but the tension in my shoulders and the nagging beginnings of a headache started up. "How about something relaxing?" I asked. "Do you have anything for tension headaches?"

Lily's eyes widened with concern. "You have a headache, Dakota?"

I nodded. "There are a lot of things swirling around me right now. Normally I drink coffee, but maybe this morning I can try something new."

Lily nodded. "I'd recommend a green tea," she said. "I don't want to make you sleepy, so I shouldn't give you anything with Lemon Balm or Chamomile." She looked back at the wide variety of tea displayed neatly on the back wall. "How do you feel about mint?"

I shrugged. "I like mint."

Lily pulled down a few glass jars of loose herbs and quickly mixed some things together.

"Skullcap?" I inquired as I read the label on one of the pretty square jars.

She gave me a mysterious smile. "Trust me," she said. "I went to school for this." Lily looked up at me, her eyes twinkling with amusement.

I snorted and let her do her thing. "As long as I don't fall asleep at the register, I'll drink whatever you give me."

Lily waved me away, and I walked over to lean against the old brick wall right next to the pickup station. A few minutes later, Lily handed me a steaming paper cup. "Here."

I handed her a five-dollar bill, and she shook her head. "On the house this morning. If you like it and it helps, let me know, please. I'm always looking to add new brews to the menu."

"Thanks so much!" I took a sip, pleasantly surprised at the subtle hint of mint and the earthiness of the tea.

"There's milk and sugar at the back if you want to add it in." She studied me for a moment, her delicate brows furrowed. "I heard a rumor..." she began.

I sighed. "About Cole?"

She shook her head. "About you." One of her shoulders lifted in a shrug. "A little about Cole, but you're here so I can ask you. You two... are you involved?"

I blinked at her. She was asking me for more reasons than curiosity. "Uh. No," I said after a moment. "We're just friends." My stomach lurched as I said it when I realized why Lily was asking me.

She nodded, but her eyes had a knowing look. "He is a good man," she pronounced suddenly.

My heart constricted, but I nodded. "He is," I agreed.

Lily smiled. "It's difficult to know one's own heart. Once we discover it, things become a lot clearer."

My fingers tightened around the cup. I didn't want to talk about this anymore. "Thank you for the tea, Lily," I said.

"You're welcome. Please let me know if there's anything else I can do for you."

I nodded and rushed out of the shop.

SEVEN

I looked around the interior of Tattered Pages and realized I hadn't done a single thing to decorate for the holiday season. I'd decorated for fall, but we were sliding right into winter and the entire town square was already decked out for Christmas. My shop was the lone holdout. I opened up the shop, flipped the sign to Open, and set Poppy down who promptly ran off.

I could put twinkling lights in the window. I tapped my finger on my chin as I looked around the store. It came to me like a lightning bolt. "I can make a book tree!" I exclaimed in the sudden silence. A startled yowl from Poppy made me laugh out loud. "Sorry, cat!" I called out even as my mind started racing with the possibilities. I could make it from the ground up using green books with different colored spines. But did I have enough? I'd have to think about it. Then I could do a tree with open white books at the top for the tree topper. My mind spun with the possibilities, and I grinned. I had the perfect spot right at the front of the store or I could even do a window display. Harriet's display flashed in my mind and my competitive nature came out.

Harper still wasn't back, but there were no customers right now. I'd get started this morning and work on it throughout the day. Cole still lurked in the back of my mind, but I still hadn't thought about how I was going to start trying to figure out who killed Lindsay.

A FEW HOURS later I was surrounded by a massive pile of colorful books and an empty window display. The bell over the door jangled, and I started to stand when Hardy walked in. I frowned at him and plopped back down on the floor.

"Hardy," I acknowledged, my voice grumpy despite me trying to play it cool.

"Dakota," he said, his tone full of amusement.

"I don't see what's so funny this morning," I griped. "You've taken an innocent man into custody."

Hardy sighed and came over to where I sat. "What's going on here?"

"Decorating for the holidays. Sort of."

"Do you need any help?"

I looked up at him, my lips twisted in a frown. He smelled freshly showered and had brought the scent of winter inside with him. His dark hair was freshly combed away from his face and his blue eyes sparkled as he looked down at me. Hardy wasn't wearing his uniform this morning.

"Are you off today?"

He nodded. "For the next two days, actually."

"And you just left Cole?" Horror filled me at the thought of Cole sitting in a jail cell by himself.

Hardy shook his head. "He should be out on bail soon. I can't do much for him right now. But that isn't why I'm here." Hardy sat on the floor in front of me and picked up one of the books. "A Christmas Cookbook," he recited out loud and showed me the front cover. "Are these all Christmas books?"

"No. They're mostly green, though."

Hardy's eyebrows went up. "Want to fill me in?"

I leaned back and looked at him. "Why are you so interested?"

Instead of getting angry, he grinned at me. "You're adorable when you're grumpy."

My look grew thunderous. "I am not grumpy!" I snapped.

His grin grew even wider. He spread his hands out. "I don't want to fight with you. If you really think about it, you know I'm not the enemy here. I'm only doing my job."

I gently set the book I was holding down and rubbed my eyes. "I know." I admitted. "But I don't like seeing people I care about get treated the way you treated him."

"I treated him better than the local authorities would have," he reminded me gently. "I allowed him to keep his pride."

I chewed my lip for a moment. Being angry at Hardy wasn't easy, and I knew my behavior was borderline irrational. "I'm sorry," I admitted finally.

"You have nothing to apologize for," Hardy said after a surprised pause.

"Stop being so nice to me," I groused.

Hardy laughed and held up another book. "Now tell me what we're doing here, and I'll help you."

AS IT TURNED OUT, making peace with a six-foot detective ensured I got an enormous and sturdy Christmas book tree. My five-foot something height would never have been able to make a book tree as high as Hardy got it without the use of a ladder. With no one here to spot me, it could have been a disaster in the making.

He stacked the last of the white books at the top and put an angel book cover out as a final touch. "Are you sure you're going to have enough books to sell?" he asked once it was finished.

The shelves had taken quite a beating once I had this brilliant idea. "I have a shipment coming in later this week," I told him. "I made a larger order than usual with Christmas coming up. A lot of people will be in here shopping for more than just regular things, so I ordered calendars for the new year, along with journals and some exercise books."

Hardy laughed, a bright and happy sound. "Ah yes, the old I'm going to get in the best shape of my life promise." He nodded sagely. "I've made that promise a few times before."

"Me too," I admitted, but I still hadn't lost the extra weight around my hips. It followed me no matter how careful I was with what I ate. But this time of year always made it even more difficult, especially since Trudy's shop was in the same strip mine was. I found it way too easy to go over there and sample all the goodies she had. When she came up with new things, I was a goner.

I studied the tree. "I need lights."

"And ornaments," Hardy added. "What do you think about garland?"

I shrugged a shoulder. "I'm anti-garland, unless it's natural."

"Like pinecones and cranberries?"

"Yup. Something with snow would be super cute, but I don't have time to run to the craft store today."

"You still have time before the holidays really kick into high gear," Hardy said. Silverwood Hollow got a little weird around Christmas time. We were all in about two-and-a-half weeks until Christmas. Carolers, decorations, sledding in the street, ice skating at the manmade rink. This place would turn into a winter wonderland soon enough.

I was glad I decided not to put the display in the window. It wouldn't have worked anyway once we went over the four-foot mark. It met people as soon as they came into the store, so I wanted to make sure I made it as ostentatious as possible. Lights would be the first thing. Then I planned to make a contest where whoever guessed how many books were actually in the pile would win a $50 gift certificate to my store and a free scone at Trudy's shop. Once I asked her, of course.

Hardy stretched, the lean muscles in his arm flexing as he reached for the ceiling. It had been nice spending this time with him. We didn't talk about Cole or murder or much of anything else. We focused solely on building the book tree. He worked with a methodical process I enjoyed watching and was able to make sure the tree stayed structurally sound. The last thing I needed was someone to walk in here and get buried under a massive pile of books.

I'd actually bought Hardy something a few weeks ago, and even though he was in here hanging out, I hesitated to give it to him. It wasn't anything overly special, but I'd thought about him when I saw it and purchased it on a whim. I'd tucked it under the register in a craft bag with a red ribbon. But now, I felt like maybe if I did give it to him, it would take our relationship in a weird direction. We weren't at the stage of Christmas gifts yet.

Sometimes I didn't even like him that much. Yesterday being a perfect example. But today... today I saw a man I wouldn't mind having in my life. The thought of it sent a chill down my spine. I didn't want to be one of those women pining over a man I couldn't have.

"What?" he asked, one of his dark eyebrows raised.

I blinked and realized I'd been staring at him for too long. "Nothing," I said quickly.

"It's definitely something, Dakota. Your ears were almost smoking."

That dragged a reluctant smile out of me. "I got you something," I admitted.

His head tilted, interest sparking in his gaze. "Oh?"

"I bought it before you arrested Cole!" I grumped.

Hardy snorted in amusement. "And you were trying to figure out whether I deserved it?"

I'd been doing exactly that. My lips twitched with amusement and when Hardy's eyebrow rose, I started to laugh.

"That's exactly what you were doing!" He grinned at me and looked back at the book tree. "So, does my manual labor this morning make up for everything yesterday?"

It didn't, but I knew this was not Hardy's fault. He'd done the best he could with what he had. Holding up a finger, I walked behind the register and took out the bag.

"Here." I shoved it at him unceremoniously. "It's nothing."

Hardy took the bag from me. At first, he merely held it, his expression something I couldn't decipher. He shook it first.

I gasped. "Hardy!"

He gave me an unrepenting grin. "So, it's breakable then?"

A mock glare darkened my face. "You should never shake a present someone's given you. It's bad manners."

"My deepest apologies," he said sincerely. Hardy took the tissue paper out of the bag and pulled out what I'd bought him. His breath caught in his throat. "Dakota. This is amazing." His startled blue gaze met mine.

I smiled. "I saw it when I went out of town and thought you might like it."

"I love it." He finished unwrapping the set of older books and set the other two down on the register. Carefully, he opened the first one and skimmed the copyright page.

I couldn't afford the first edition of the books. Few people could. The leather-bound Sherlock Holmes books were published in the late 1800s and were signed by the author. Hardy did exactly what I hoped he'd do. He handled the books with reverence, awe written all over his face.

He'd never told me he liked Sherlock Holmes, but I'd seen his office a couple of times and he had the newer editions of the books on his credenza behind his chair. I'd gone into another rare books' supplier a few towns over and since I'd made such a huge purchase, they threw in the Sherlock Holmes books for a pretty price.

"I'm not sure I should accept these," Hardy said after a moment.

My heart plummeted to the ground. "Why not?"

His mouth opened and shut. "Because," he finally said, "these must have cost a pretty penny." Hardy scratched the back of his neck. "And I didn't get you anything."

"First of all," I said as I tried my best not to be irritated, "that is not the point of gift giving. I got you a gift because I wanted to. Not because I wanted you to get me something. Second of all, I deal in rare books. I know what they're worth, but I also know how to get a good deal. If you don't want them, you can leave them here, but I bought them for you."

He stared down at the books. "This is the best gift anyone has ever gotten me."

Something struck my heart then. "It was my pleasure. I saw you had some of his books on your credenza, so I thought you might like these."

"Should I handle them with gloves or keep them stored somewhere temperature controlled?"

"It's up to you. I wouldn't handle them too often. You can keep them in your office if you aren't worried about them getting stolen."

Hardy snorted. "I would hope no one would be brave enough to get light fingered in a police station."

"You never know."

Hardy put the books down and stepped closer to me. "Thank you, Dakota." He held his arms out, and I stepped into them without a second thought. The moment his arms closed around me, I realized how well we fit together.

Danger, Dakota, I thought. *Danger!*

He gave me a quick squeeze and stepped away. "I'm due somewhere for lunch, so I have to run." Hardy carefully wrapped the books back up and put them in the bag. "Let me know if you need any more help with the book tree."

I waved at him as he headed out of the shop. "Thanks for the help!"

"Any time." The bell over the door jingled as he walked

out and suddenly the shop was quiet as a tomb without his presence.

Poppy decided to make her presence known just then. She curled around my feet, so I reached down and scratched her on top of the head. "You didn't want to visit today?" I asked.

Poppy meowed but continued winding through my legs until I eventually sat on the floor. She hopped into my lap, content for a moment, and I scratched her behind the ears. This was a rarity with her, and I knew if I pet her a hint too little or too much, she'd repay me with a clawed swipe. Such was life with cats.

I SPENT the rest of the day checking out customers. The afternoon had picked up some but overall, it was still a slow day. Everyone who'd come in commented on the book tree. I'd set up a glass fishbowl with a notepad and a pencil next to it to start taking entries for the contest.

"Make sure you put a good number where I can reach you," I told the woman filling one out. "Just in case you win I need to be able to get a hold of you."

Everyone loved a good contest.

The day passed by with little incident until right before closing time. Two women walked in. Both were young, but they had a big city look about them. One wore a pair of wide legged slacks with a white tucked in blouse and heels so high they put her over six feet. The other wore a suit that reminded me of Lindsay's. She wore a red pencil skirt with a high-necked black blouse.

"Welcome to Tattered Pages," I greeted. Both of them ignored me and went straight to the biography section.

The shop was small, and no other customers were in today so I could overhear their conversation without even trying.

"I can't believe we were sent here for this nonsense," said the blonde in the pants. "Lindsay knew what she was doing was dangerous."

The one in the skirt snorted. "Rare books aren't dangerous, Sid."

The blonde stared at her open mouthed. "Chloe. Are you serious? You didn't hear what she was doing?"

Chloe shrugged. "I don't get into office gossip as much as you do."

Sid rolled her eyes. "It's not office gossip. Everyone knew she was taking money and funneling it into a project in this godforsaken town."

I perked up at that and leaned in just enough to hear a little better.

"This town?" Chloe looked around. "What could *possibly* be happening in this little town?"

I bristled at that one. A lot happened in Silverwood Hollows.

"She wanted to start a spa." Sid shrugged. "Some kind of hoity toity place that catered to rich tourists. But rare books don't make good money."

I snorted at that one. People had killed for less.

Sid leaned in and lowered her voice, but I could still hear her. "She was faking books and pretending she was sourcing them from legitimate collectors, then selling to the people dumb enough to not double check if they were the real deal."

Chloe's delicate eyebrows rose. "She'd risk her reputation for that?"

"She didn't care. All she wanted was to start that spa. Lindsay never really cared all that much about those books. She got into it because her family did."

"How much money had she stolen?" Chloe asked.

I wanted to know too.

"Not enough," Sid said. "Last I heard, she was having trouble securing the right permits to even break ground."

"Hmmm," Chloe said. "And now she's gone. Someone must have figured out what she was doing."

"They have a man in custody," Sid said.

They had to be talking about Cole. I held my breath. I needed to know what was going on with him and Lindsay. Even though Cole said it wasn't important, it had to be. She wouldn't have wound up dead right afterward if not. Maybe Cole knew she was stealing. If that's the case, maybe he was doing a story on her, or the people involved in this. It couldn't have been just her. Could it? Usually, one person wasn't smart enough to make a con that big. "He's handsome," Chloe whispered.

How would she know that?

"I heard he's a reporter for the local paper," Sid said. "Curious he'd be tangled up with her." Sid snorted. "Or not curious at all if you knew Lindsay. She got her hooks into a lot of people."

"You shouldn't speak ill of the dead," Chloe said, an uncomfortable look on her face.

Sid rolled her eyes. "She's not here to hear it."

They browsed through the biographies for a while until they eventually found their way to the romance section. I nonchalantly wandered over to them. "Are you looking for anything special?"

Sid looked me up and down and immediately dismissed me. Chloe gave me an embarrassed smile. "Um. Do you have any Danielle Steel?"

I nodded. "Sure do. I carry more of her older works than her newer. Is there something you had in mind?"

"I've heard *Message from 'Nam* is really good," she said.

I motioned for her to follow me. "It's one of my favorites." I showed her where we kept the Danielle Steel books and pointed to an area close by. "If you've never read Jackie Collins, I'd recommend her too. She's spicier and a lot of her books deal with the mafia."

Chloe's eyes widened. "Ooh. Those sound great." She beelined for the Jackie Collins' books, and I headed back over to where Sid was. She seemed to be the one with all the information. "I'll be right over there if you need anything. I hope you're enjoying your stay in Silverwood Hollow."

Sid sighed. "It's alright. Are there any good dress up places to go?"

"Dress up places?" My brow crinkled. "I'm not sure what you mean."

Sid huffed. "You know. Where I can wear more than a pair of jeans and work boots?"

Annoyance reared its ugly head inside of me. I smiled politely. "We operate on a more farm-to-table sustainable basis. There are some wonderful restaurants on the outskirts of town and there's another just a few streets over. Most things around here are on a come as you are basis because we're all family around here." I gave her a toothy smile. "If you'll excuse me, I'll be over by the register. Just head on over when you're ready to check out."

Sid's eyes narrowed. She knew I was insulting her, but she couldn't figure out how yet. It might take her a while.

A little while later, Chloe dumped seven books on the register. Sid followed her and had exactly none. No surprise there. I didn't take her for a reader. I chastised myself mentally for being judgmental. It didn't matter if she read or not. I'd still take customers however they came in and Chloe had just bought enough to make a nice little cha-ching sound go off in my head.

Chloe paid in cash and grinned at me as I handed over the bag. "Let me know how you like it," I said, finding myself relieved they were leaving.

"I sure will!" she said cheerily. Sid looked back at me, a thoughtful look on her face before she walked out.

We might be a small town, but assuming we were bumpkins wouldn't be too smart on Sid's part.

I HEADED over to Trudy's once I closed up the shop, hoping I had enough willpower to say no to her delicious offerings. I did, however, grab a cup of straight coffee and motioned her over to the table when she saw me. As soon as she sat down, she blew a strand of bright red hair out of her face. "Woo," she said and blew out a breath. "Today has been a heck of a day." She gave me an appraising look. "The rumor mill is positively abuzz about how long Hardy stayed in your shop today."

I groaned. "He was helping me set up a book tree today." I pointed at myself. "Me short. Hardy tall. Book tree tall."

Trudy chuckled. "I didn't say it was me, but I got a little curious myself. Especially when I saw him walk out clutching something like it was the most precious thing ever given to him."

I didn't want to talk about it but knew I had to give her something to change the subject. "He's a fan of Sherlock Holmes so I found him a set for his office."

Her eyebrows wiggled, but she didn't press it. "Say, did you see two women today all dressed up like they were from New York or something?"

I rolled my eyes. "I did. They came into the bookshop."

"Those two gossiped like old hens!" Trudy leaned back in her chair. "All they could talk about was that woman who died."

"Lindsay. I think the company she worked for sent them over here. No idea why."

"She didn't say." Trudy shook her head. "But I have a bad feeling about those two. They seem like trouble. Especially that blonde one."

"Sid?" I inquired.

"That's it. Sid. She seemed like a snake."

"That one will definitely sneak up and bite you in the back," I agreed.

Silence fell between us. "Cole was arrested," Trudy said. It was a statement and not a question.

"Sort of. Hardy came by his house and picked him up last night."

A hard look stole over her face. "I like Hardy, but I don't like it when he obviously has the wrong guy, and he won't look anywhere else." She snorted with disgust.

Part of me wanted to defend him but I knew where she was coming from. "I don't think he has a choice with this one. Cole is the only evidence he has right now."

She shook her head. "It doesn't seem right. Someone had to have seen something. It was broad daylight for crying out loud!"

"Lots of things happen during broad daylight that go unnoticed. I agree, though. Someone getting bludgeoned over the head couldn't have been a quiet thing." I winced as I said it. Someone probably took her by surprise. There was no way she wouldn't have screamed if someone came at her with something.

Unless she knew them.

I sat up a little straighter. That didn't look good for Cole. They definitely knew each other. Trudy and I locked gazes. "Do you think it was someone in this town? Someone we know?" Fear rose in her eyes.

"I don't want to get ahead of myself. Lindsay was involved in some pretty shady stuff from what I gather." I was so glad I left before I listened to the rest of her pitch. Thinking about it now, I thought I might need to reach out to Harriet and have her contact anyone Lindsay successfully pitched to. That way we could figure out exactly what she was doing. Or at least get one step closer to unraveling this puzzle.

"There's no easy way to go about this," Trudy said. "Are you looking into it?"

I blinked at her, surprised. "Why do you assume I'm looking into it?"

Trudy laughed. "Because you're Dakota. And you solved our last murder," she said.

I held my hands up. "I did no such thing!" I protested.

"You certainly helped. Everyone here knows it."

I really didn't know how much I helped. I stumbled through and wandered around the clues and eventually found myself in a terrifying situation that I wasn't sure I'd get out of. Regardless, the murder was solved, and I did receive some credit, but the entire thing made me uncomfortable.

"Cole is in trouble," I said. A sigh escaped me, and Trudy reached over and took my hand.

"He needs your help. We both know he didn't kill her."

"He won't tell me what they were arguing about. It's weird. He's in jail for murder and he still won't tell me what happened."

A thoughtful look stole over her face. "Were they involved?"

"Intimately?" I shrugged. "I don't know. It seems like it. I just don't know."

Trudy and I sat in silence for a moment. "Do you think you should try to get Chloe alone?"

My eyebrows went up. "That's not a bad idea. But she didn't know as much as Sid did."

Her nose wrinkled. "Sid seems like she's super fun at a party."

The sarcasm dripping from that statement made me laugh. "She is pretty mean. But she knew Cole had been arrested and I'm not sure how considering she's not from this town." I sat up straight. "Do you think someone is feeding her information?"

Trudy's lips thinned. "This is a tight knit town. I wouldn't think so."

"I thought it was too, but we've had two murders in only a few months. I wonder if we're as close as we used to be."

"Silverwood Hollow folks will always stick together. No matter what happens, we're going to talk to each other and stick together."

The hopeful part of me wanted to believe that. The logical part of me wondered if there was a larger conspiracy going around. Something just under the surface that we couldn't see. "I hope so." I drained the rest of my coffee and stood. "I'm going to see if I can track those women down."

Trudy laughed. "Check the local bar." She rolled her eyes. "They were on the way to try to find martinis."

A snort escaped me as I thought about them trying to find martinis and cosmos in Silverwood Hollow. "Their best bet is Mac's."

She nodded. "He'll try to make anything. It doesn't mean it will be good."

I slung my purse over my shoulder. "I'll head there right now."

"Let me know how it goes," Trudy said.

"I'll pop by tomorrow."

"Just in time for the unveiling of my new hot chocolate!"

"You just did one!" I griped. "My waistline can't handle all your delicious inventions."

"Your will is weak," Trudy teased. "The hot chocolate is wearing down your willpower."

"Until tomorrow," I said dramatically as I headed out the door. "Please make this one a diet hot chocolate."

"Sure," Trudy said. "I'll get right on that."

MAC'S WAS a dive bar just on the edge of town. The parking lot was full and country music trickled out from beneath the old wooden door. I stood at the entrance wondering if this was something I really wanted to do. I hadn't been in a bar in forever. Not since I was in my twenties and it was dollar beer night in college. I cringed in embarrassment years later over that and thanked everything that was holy that I'd grown up and managed to get some sense. Bars weren't really my thing. I didn't drink a lot, and I certainly didn't frequent places where people drank too much and threw sharp objects at a board with numbers on it.

Squaring my shoulders, I pushed open the door and was immediately met with the acrid scent of cigarette smoke and spilled beer. This was a bad idea. But just as soon as I decided to turn right back around, my gaze fell on Chloe and Sid, dressed to the nines and pretending they knew how to play pool. I sighed and walked all the way in. At first, I didn't know where to go so I made a beeline for the bar.

Mac stood behind the counter, a towel slung over his wide shoulder. His eyes widened comically when he saw me.

"Hey Dakota," he said once he'd shaken off his surprise. "Is there something I can do for you?"

I forced a smile on my face. "I'd like a ..." My voice trailed off. I had no idea what to order.

His grey bushy eyebrows lifted and for a second a confused furrow lit his brow. Then his expression cleared as if he knew why I was here. I didn't know how I felt about that.

"How about a Shirley Temple?" he asked.

I had no idea what that was, so I nodded. He snorted. "If someone asks you what that is, you tell 'em it's a cranberry and vodka, okay?"

I nodded eagerly. "Okay."

A minute later, I held a pink and clear drink with a tiny little umbrella in it. Trepidation filled me as I took a sip. I'd driven here, and I didn't want to be tipsy and drive. Maybe I should have downloaded that app. Whatever it was. *Loober* or something. I made my way closer to Chloe and Sid. They were surrounded by four men I'd never seen before. Men who seemed like they weren't from this town. Two of them wore black slacks and loosened ties over their button-down shirts. Their hair was slicked back, and their faces were clean shaven. They looked fresh out of college and flush with Daddy's money. The other two looked a little more like blue-collar men. Five o'clock shadow, blue jeans and t-shirts. Those two didn't talk to the clean-cut men, so I wondered if they knew each other or if they were both vying for Chloe and Sid's attention. I chose a table just a few feet away and settled in to see what I could hear.

Unfortunately, the music was too loud. George Jones talked about a love that died and the clack of balls on the pool table obscured any kind of conversation. Annoyed, I sipped my drink and tried to figure out how to sidle closer to them so I could hear what was going on. Short of going up to them and pretending to be their friend, I was pretty much out of options.

A few minutes later, I locked eyes with Chloe. I pretended like I was surprised to see her and widened my eyes and waved. "Chloe!" I called. "So nice to see you here!"

It was only then that I remembered she'd never introduced herself. Her gaze narrowed for a moment but cleared almost immediately, probably thanks to the pink drink she held in her manicured hand.

"You're the bookstore lady!" she called back. Chloe waved me over, and I picked up my drink and rushed over before she changed her mind.

The scent of sweet alcohol was on her breath. Chloe slung an arm over my shoulders. "Sid! Hey Sid!"

Sid rolled her eyes but sidled up to us. She wore a black mini dress and a face full of makeup. Her blue eyes were lined with black eyeliner and her hair was teased at least two inches higher than it normally sat. "So, it's the bookstore lady. I must admit, I didn't expect to see you in a place like this."

"I've had a tough night," I admitted. "And home was a lonely place to go."

Sid's gaze narrowed. "You can sit with us. I guess." Her tone was begrudging, but she made room for me at their table.

I gratefully took a seat. Sid was drinking some kind of clear drink and there were a few discarded empty glasses in front of the full one she had. Maybe it would be much easier to get them talking than it would have been earlier. But I couldn't do it now. I had to wait for a little while until they got a little more comfortable with me.

Chloe swayed on her feet. "So," she slurred a little. "Tell me. Are you dating anyone?"

A nervous laugh escaped me. "Uh no. There's no one I'm interested in right now." I'm so glad I wasn't hooked up to a lie detector machine because it would have blared out to the world I was a big, fat liar.

Chloe's eyes widened comically. "No one?" She picked up a lock of my dark hair. "But look at this! You're sooooo pretty!"

She twirled a strand around her finger. "Rhett!" she called. "Isn't ..." she paused. "What's your name?"

"Dakota," I supplied.

"Isn't Dakota soooo pretty?" She fluffed my hair.

Rhett turned and grunted. "She's pretty hot," he said and gave me a closer look.

I squirmed under his intense gaze not liking where this was going.

"Cameron!"

"That's okay," I told her. "Thank you, though."

"Cameron! Look at my friend. Isn't she gorgeous!" Cameron, the other guy in slacks, looked my way. He shrugged. "Not as hot as you are."

Chloe preened under his attention. "Aww. Thanks, Cam."

The other two guys were staring at me now. I looked down and studied my Shirley Temple. "So," I said, tracing the rim of my drink. "How long are you two in town?"

Sid snorted. "We're here until we figure out where our co-worker hid something."

Chloe giggled. "You aren't supposed to tell anyone that," she said in a stage whisper.

"I don't think there's anything. They've sent us on a wild

goose chase." Sid took a sip of her drink. "But Lindsay had a lot of secrets, so who knows."

Chloe's face fell. "It's so sad she died."

"She didn't die, Chloe. Someone murdered her," Sid snapped. "Dying implies she passed away in her sleep."

By then a couple of the surrounding guys were beginning to look uncomfortable.

"What about that Cole guy?" I asked as I twirled the umbrella in my drink.

"He's soooo cute," Chloe said dramatically.

Sid eyed me and I wondered if she was as tipsy as she seemed. "You live here. You don't know him?"

"I know of him." I looked down. "He's come into my shop a couple of times, but I've never said more than a hello to him."

"I'd like to get his number," Chloe interjected.

"He's out on bail right now," Sid said. "Shoot your shot, girl."

"Do you think he was involved with Lindsay?" I shook my head. "It's all so sad. Things like this don't happen around here."

"Things like this happen everywhere. You never know what lengths some people will go to." Sid got up and picked her pool cue up leaving me and Chloe alone at the table.

"What do you think?" I asked Chloe. "Were they seeing each other?"

She stirred her drink with the straw. "I don't think Lindsay had a boyfriend, but she and I didn't talk much. The last time I saw her, she was buying a car." Chloe frowned. "But it was kinda weird. She had a huge bag full of cash."

I blinked. "Cash?"

Chloe swayed on her seat. "Yeah. I was in there with a guy I used to date. He bought a new car like every few months." She rolled her eyes and tossed her hair over her shoulder. "I had to go to the bathroom, and I passed by a room where the door was cracked. I heard Lindsay's voice and peeked in." She giggled. "I'm so nosy."

I wanted to yell at her to keep talking, but I smiled encouragingly.

"Lindsay was in there with one of the salesmen and she had this big black bag full of bundled cash." Chloe leaned in. "I've never seen that much cash in my life."

"Did she buy the car?"

Chloe blinked. "No idea. I just assumed she did. After that, she came here, and I hadn't seen her since."

Interesting. My mind spun with all the possibilities. People involved in legitimate business ventures usually didn't carry around huge bags of cash. It was more than I had this morning. I reached over and patted her hand. "I'm really sorry about your friend."

"She wasn't my friend. Just a coworker. I can't believe she's dead, though. I just saw her a little while ago."

"Did she seem off or anything?" I probably pushed too hard because Chloe's brow furrowed.

"Like what do you mean?"

"Upset. Frazzled. Not herself?"

"Why are you so curious about her?" Chloe asked, suspicion beginning to form on her face.

I smiled. "It's a small town. I want to feel safe here and just want to know if I still need to worry about anything. The person who killed her is still out there."

"I don't think you have anything to worry about," Chloe said glumly.

I paused my stirring. "Why's that?"

"Sid says Lindsay got what was coming to her."

I dropped all talk about Lindsay after that statement and tried to figure out how to extricate myself from the table. Sid might not have murdered her, but it sounded like she knew who did. I needed to talk to Hardy but talking to him would reveal I'd been asking around about Lindsay. He'd be angry at me, but it would take some of the suspicion off Cole.

Sid wandered back over to the table and sat down next to Chloe. She noticed the lull in conversation. "Why so broody?" Sid nudged Chloe who said nothing.

"We were just talking about what happened." I stood to go. "I'm just nervous about there being a killer still loose." Holding up my drink, I waved it. "I'm going to meet up with a friend. Appreciate you chatting with me!"

I turned to go, but Sid cleared her throat. "Hey Dakota?"

I stopped. "Yes?"

"I think you're safe. No need to worry about Lindsay. I'd just be careful not to draw too much attention to yourself."

It sounded like a threat. I opened my mouth to speak only to realize there wasn't anything I could say to that. Instead, I smiled and gave her a short nod. "Have a good night, ladies."

Chloe's wide eyes stuck with me for a while after I'd left.

"HARPER, WHAT'S A SHIRLEY TEMPLE?" I asked my assistant. I was so glad to have her back. Sleeping in for another hour this morning was the best thing to happen to me in weeks.

She snorted and paused in her paperwork. "It's a non-alcoholic drink. Why?"

I laughed out loud. Mac had bamboozled me. "I went to a bar a few nights ago and didn't know what to order. Mac gave me one and told me if anyone asked what it was to say it was a vodka and cranberry."

A dimple peeked out from her cheek as she grinned at me. "That's honestly wholesome. Mac's good people."

"Yeah," I agreed. "He sure is. It tasted good, too." I suspected the drink had no alcohol in it before I'd even left the bar. I couldn't taste anything inside of it and felt no different from when I walked in. Good thing, too. Sid's words had lifted the hair right off the back of my neck and I hadn't been able to sleep since.

She knew something. How much I didn't know, but she was hiding something. Hardy and I hadn't seen each other since he'd helped me put up the tree, and while I planned to go to him as soon as I got out of the bar, Sid's chilling last words gave me pause. I couldn't help but feel like she was watching me. Or someone was. If I went to the police, I'd be a target. Or maybe that's just what she wanted me to think.

Regardless, something was rotten in Denmark. Lindsay showing up with a huge bag of money, Sid and Chloe here looking for something she supposedly hid, and Cole's argument leading up to her death all made me feel like there was something much more sinister at play here.

I knew I needed to go. Not going would mean withholding evidence from an investigation and that was a crime. I couldn't hold off much longer.

Cole had dropped off the face of the planet since his release on bail. I checked my cell daily but there were no calls or texts from him. I wanted to reach out to him, but I wasn't sure if he'd welcome it. His last words were a plea for my help and being seen with him could jeopardize him.

I scrubbed a hand over my face and let out a sigh.

Poppy just then came over and hopped up on the register area.

"Hey, Poppy."

She butted me with her head and looked to the romance section. I scratched her behind the ears. She did it again and once again looked over to that section. I stilled and watched her. Poppy and I locked eyes just before she hopped down and walked away. She stopped before she was out of sight and looked back at me, as if asking me to follow.

Harper watched Poppy for a moment. "She's acting strange, isn't she?"

"She is." I walked out from behind the register. Poppy had

good instincts. If she was asking me to follow her, I'd entertain her.

She led me to the romance section and deeper into the stacks. Then she stopped abruptly right next to a small slip of paper on the floor. I bent down to pick it up and Poppy yowled at me.

When I opened it, I saw a note and a phone number. Scrawled in neat cursive were the words, "Meet me at 2409 Silverwood Maple Lane. 7 p.m."

The note was signed by Lindsay.

My mouth dropped open. Poppy stared at me unblinkingly. "Holy smokes, Poppy. You're a genius." I wasn't sure what I could do with the note, if anything, but this was definitely a clue. I had cameras installed a while ago. After Marcy's murder, I didn't feel safe anywhere. The cameras had given me more security, and they came in handy when I needed to check on some things. When I first got them, I'd forget to turn them on, but I made it into a habit where everything first happened. Now I did my best to make sure I checked them every single day. It didn't always happen, but I tried.

"I wish you could talk," I muttered to her. "It sure would be nice to know when this was dropped and who dropped it." It had to be either Chloe's or Sid's note. I was leaning toward Sid. She seemed to know a lot more than Chloe did. But I wasn't looking forward to going through days of footage either. I could narrow it down to the day, but I'd have to skip through a lot of boring footage before I found what I needed.

If I could connect this to Sid, it's possible Hardy could narrow the suspect list. Although if he had a list, I'd be surprised, especially since Cole was on the hook for it right now. If the note was sent to Sid from Lindsay, Sid might just be the killer.

I tucked the note into my pocket and hurried into the back office. It was now or never.

I had to call Hardy when it wasn't too late.

His voicemail picked up after the second ring. I didn't leave a message. Instead I hung up and made a mental note to try him first thing in the morning.

I'd rather avoid talking to him if I could, but since he'd been so adamant about me staying out of this, I figured it was the least I could do.

EIGHT

The next morning, Hardy answered his phone on the first ring with a brusque, "Cavanaugh."

"This is Dakota."

"Everything okay?" he said, sounding all at once alert.

"Everything is fine, but I have information for you."

He sighed, a deep and drawn-out sound. "Dakota…"

"You arrested Cole. I'm not going to stay out of it."

"You will if I arrested you for obstructing justice."

"It's not obstructing justice when you provide evidence proving someone else might be the killer!"

"I'm listening," he ground out.

"I found a note dropped in the bookstore. I think it was from a couple of days ago. Two women from out of town were in here and they both knew Lindsay. They said something about their company flying them in. I have no idea why they're here, but one of them mentioned trying to find something Lindsay was hiding."

"Go on." Hardy did not seem enthused about taking this information from me. Maybe he was jealous I found it out before he could.

"Well, when I went to the bar -"

"You did WHAT?" Hardy exploded. "You purposely went to a bar where these women were hanging out even knowing they could be dangerous?"

"It's a public bar, Hardy."

"And no crimes ever happen in public." Irritation was palpable in his voice. "You can't keep doing this, Dakota. It's dangerous."

"I'm aware. But I'm not going to let Cole go down for something he didn't do!"

Hardy sighed over the line. "You don't trust me, do you?"

I blinked in surprise. Silence fell over the line. "Of course I do," I blurted, but the silence had gone on too long, and I'd hesitated.

"You don't. Did you think I enjoyed arresting Cole?"

"No," I said, but I wondered if he had. He and Cole didn't get along.

"I may not like Cole, but it has nothing to do with this investigation. I'm a professional and *impartial* officer of the law. I go where the evidence takes me. I'm trained to do this. I know how to follow clues, connect the pieces of the puzzle, and arrest the right person."

"I know that."

"Do you?" he asked, his voice beginning to rise. "You have no experience in investigations. No experience in murder. No weapons training. No negotiation training and you have no idea how to question potential suspects. You're blindly stumbling into my investigations and trying to find clues where there are none!"

Tears stung the back of my eyes. "I'm only trying to help," I insisted. "Did you already know this?"

"It doesn't matter if I did or not. What matters is you staying out of police investigations."

"It does matter. I'm not doing anything wrong. *Cole* didn't do anything wrong, and he was falsely arrested."

"Careful, Dakota," Hardy warned. "That sounds very close to you accusing me of wrongdoing."

The tension over the line grew between us. In that moment, I felt like our relationship had fractured. Gone was the easy banter between us. Now it was him against me. Or at least it felt like it.

"I will do anything to help my friends," I said at last. "I haven't impeded you in any way or endangered myself."

"Stepping into a murder investigation means you endangered yourself immediately. The second you put yourself in front of those two women was the second you became interesting to them. And you know what happens to interesting people when it comes to murder?" He didn't wait for my response. "They wind up dead."

I opened my mouth to give him a piece of my mind, but he spoke first.

"Goodbye, Dakota. This is the last warning I'm going to give you. Stay out of my investigations." The line clicked.

Hardy Cavanaugh had just hung up on me.

ANGER still bloomed in my cheeks when I walked out of my office several minutes later. He'd treated me like I was a child and assumed I'd taken no care for my safety. He couldn't be more wrong. Of course I knew it wasn't the best idea to question people about the murder, but I couldn't find anything out if I sat on my heels and waited for Hardy to do it. I already had more information than he did, and I didn't want to wait around anymore because the longer the clock ticked, the more the evidence would disappear. I picked up my cell and dialed Cole.

"You shouldn't be calling me," he said after the first ring.

"I'm glad you're out," I said, ignoring his first comment.

"Me too." I could almost hear the smile over the phone. "It wasn't so bad. Though I don't recommend the jailhouse food. The bread is stale and I'm pretty sure whatever they're using for peanut butter could peel paint from my car."

I laughed, but it was a sad sound. "I'll never serve you peanut butter again," I vowed. "Listen, I found a couple of things out. Do you know -"

"Tell me nothing, Dakota," Cole warned, his voice as serious as I'd ever heard it. "I need you to leave me out of it. I can't explain why, but please, please trust me."

"Cole, this is unfair. You asked me to help -"

"Dakota. Please. I need you to do this for me."

I sighed. "I'm not sure if this is a good idea anymore. Hardy is extremely upset with me."

"Hardy is a pain in the neck," Cole grumbled. "Though I think he's doing as much as he can to help me."

It certainly hadn't felt like it after the conversation we just had, but I'd give him the benefit of the doubt. I knew he was a good detective, but he wasn't on my good list today. "Let's hope so. When's your hearing?"

"I haven't received the date yet. I'm hoping these charges will be dismissed before that comes around." He sounded hopeful which lifted my heart a little.

"I hope so too. Maybe we can get lunch once this is all over."

"I'd like that." We said our goodbyes and just as I was about to hang up, he spoke again.

"Dakota?"

"Yes, Cole?"

"Be careful." There was an urgency in his tone I'd rarely heard before. "This isn't a case to take lightly, and I'd never forgive myself if something happened to you."

"I'm always careful." It sounded more flippant than I meant it to be.

"I'm serious. I want you to know that I think whoever is behind this is supported by some powerful people. You have a business to take care of and people who love you. Just be careful and discreet."

I cringed. Walking into a bar and coercing two drunk girls directly related to the murder was probably not the kind of discreet he meant. "I'll be the very soul of discretion," I said. *Starting tomorrow.*

I ended the call and pulled the note out of my pocket again. Next on the list was checking the security cameras, but I felt like I should visit Binders first and chat with Harriet.

"Harper, can you watch the front for a while?" I asked.

"Of course, boss." One of her eyebrows rose as she looked up at me. "Everything okay? You had the same exact look a few months ago when you got all tangled up with that Marcy business."

A hint of red touched my cheeks. I had no idea there was an "I'm impeding a murder investigation" look, but apparently, I had it. "Everything is fine! I just need to check something out that might take me a while. I'll be back as soon as I'm finished."

She nodded but didn't look convinced. "Alright then."

I gave her my best innocent look, but Harper didn't look like she was buying it.

NINE

The parking lot of Binders was mostly empty. Concern grew inside of me as I turned off the Rav 4 and got out. The lights in the shop were on and I saw a couple of people inside. Police tape still graced the parking lot, though it was mostly discarded on the ground. I would have picked it up, but I didn't want Hardy yelling at me again.

Squaring my shoulders, I took a deep breath and went inside. Harriet stood at the register, lines on her mouth where there weren't any before. Her hair wasn't as perfect as it usually was, and her shoulders slumped. Weariness was set in all of her features.

I smiled at her and walked up. "Hi Harriet."

"Dakota!" Her hand went over her heart. "You startled me."

"I'm so sorry. I thought the bell would have announced me." The bell in Tattered Pages was sometimes loud enough to wake the dead.

She shook her head and pinched the space between her brows. "Usually it would have. I've been so overwhelmed since what happened with Lindsay." A sigh escaped her. "Never in a million years would I have thought something like this would happen at my shop." Tears shone in her eyes. "And look. It's empty out there. Weekdays are usually a little slow." Her gaze met mine. "But never like this."

Empathy filled me as I took in the shop. Two customers browsed the shelves, but there was no one else in sight. "Once that police tape is gone and the crime is solved, things will get back to normal."

She looked around, her eyes pained. "I'm not sure if they will."

I reached over and took her hand briefly and squeezed. "They will. It happened for me. I got tangled up in a murder investigation a few months ago and it affected sales for a little while. I thought at first there was a bump because of all the people coming around, but it ended up being morbid curiosity."

A choked laugh escaped Harriet. "Happened to me in the first couple of days. Now people are avoiding us like the plague."

"Give it some time. There's a great detective on the case."

Harriet leaned closer. "And is it you?" she asked quietly.

I blinked in surprise. "Err. No."

Harriet's eyes widened. "Why ever not? I heard you were instrumental in solving the last crime that happened in your town."

Too many people thought this. Discomfort made me squirm. "Not really. I helped some, sure, but when it came down to it, good old-fashioned police work was what solved the case."

Harriet gave me a disbelieving look but let the matter drop. "Tell me what I can do for you," she said, changing the subject.

"I'm actually here to see if you have surveillance footage of the day Lindsay died."

"Ha!" Harriet crowed. "I knew you'd take this on! Stop being so humble, Dakota."

I held my hands up in surrender. "I'm merely helping a friend. That's all."

"Cole?" One of her eyebrows went up. "That handsome, annoying reporter?"

She'd pegged him, alright. "That's the one."

Harriet's lips thinned. "He sure seems guilty. I saw those two arguing in the parking lot."

"Did you speak to Detective Cavanaugh about it?"

Harriet nodded. "Cole came in and took a seat in the back." She sighed. "I stopped Lindsay's presentation when I realized that all she was doing was trying to sell her services. We argued for a minute or two then Cole came up and tried to intervene."

I hadn't heard this version.

"I asked her to pack up her things and leave. Lindsay demanded payment. I refused based on the fact she'd falsely portrayed her seminar as something it wasn't." She snorted in derision. "Learning opportunity, my foot."

"She got angry. *Really* angry. Cole got between us to calm us down which only made her madder." She rubbed the back of her neck. "I had to pull another employee from the office to escort her from the premises." Harriet rubbed the sides of her arms and shivered. "Bad business all the way around. Sales plummeted that day because of the argument and haven't been the same since."

"And what about Cole?" I asked. "Were they arguing in the store?"

She shook her head. "It wasn't until they stepped outside. Lindsay said something like she didn't have it yet, but she was working on it. Cole…" she swallowed hard. "Cole got really angry."

I'd seen Cole annoyed, but I don't think I'd ever seen him truly angry. "What did he say?"

"He told her they had a deal and that if she couldn't produce it, he was walking away. Lindsay really freaked out. She struck him and started screaming."

Interesting. "Could you make out what she was saying?"

"No. It was too garbled and by then they were too far away. Cole took her hands to keep her from hitting him and leaned close to say something. Lindsay looked really scared by the time they got to her car."

None of this made Cole look good. "Anything else you can remember?" I asked.

Her brow furrowed. "Someone sitting in here thought the entire thing was funny and made a comment about Lindsay's love life. Really odd. I thought they might have known each other, but the two of them didn't speak or even acknowledge each other."

"Did you catch the woman's name?"

Harriet shook her head. "No." Her eyes lit up a second later. "But I have a sign-in sheet!" She ducked below the counter. The sounds of rummaging through paper filtered above her head until she waved a piece of paper. "Ha! Found it." Harriet stood and set the paper down. She skimmed through. "I'm not too sure how to figure out who it was, but I know most of the people who showed up."

"Did you give this to Hardy?"

She shook her head. "No. I didn't even think about it." A frown turned her lips down. "As a matter of fact, he didn't even ask."

Hardy or whoever had interviewed her hadn't asked the right questions. Harriet skimmed through the paper. She made a copy of the original and marked through the names of the people she knew. When she was done, she had five names left.

"One of these is a male," she said and marked through it leaving four. "Do you want a copy of this?" she asked.

"Definitely."

Harriet handed me a copy a moment later. "Are you going to talk to any of them?"

I planned to talk to all of them if I had the time, but I didn't want anyone to know what I was doing. "Maybe," I hedged. "Do you still have the surveillance video?"

She nodded and motioned for me to follow her to the back.

WHERE THE PUBLIC area of Binders was clean and organized, the back looked more like a mad scientist's lair. Paper, boxes of books, and miscellaneous knick-knacks littered the area. Harriet led me over to a small door and into a room that looked straight out of an '80s spy movie. She shrugged and a self-deprecating smile lit her lips. "We haven't upgraded these in a while, but they work like a charm." Harriet lovingly patted the old television monitors. "Even if I could update them, I'm not sure I would. They just don't make things like they used to."

I stifled a laugh and moved closer to peer at the black and white images. Six small screens blinked back at me, the view flipping every few seconds to a new spot inside and outside of the store.

"I have cameras on all sides of the store and two indoor cameras." She chewed on her lip for a moment. "Hank switches out the tapes for me every evening."

"Tapes?" I questioned, my lips twitching.

"Hush, Dakota," she said, laughter in her voice. "We can't all be young and hip."

This time I couldn't help it. The amusement bubbled from me. "Whatever works."

She winked at me and bent down to lift a large box of VHS tapes. I hadn't seen one of those since I was in high school. My high school graduation was on a VHS tape somewhere in my mom's house, but DVDs came out the next year, so she had it placed on disc as well.

Harriet quickly flipped through the tapes until she produced one with the date of Lindsay's seminar. She peered at it and set it back in the box. "Each day usually has five or six tapes with it."

My eyebrows rose. "Do they even make those anymore?"

She shook her head. "Binders has been open for thirty-five years, honey. We have tons of video tapes we can reuse. I've had to purchase some on eBay before, but I think now we're good. As long as they hold up." Harriet grinned. "This goes back to my theory of not making things like they used to. I haven't had a single problem with any footage or any of my tapes. I'd hate to replace it with new technology when the old works fine."

I grimaced down at the stack of tapes she'd pulled out of the box. "That's all good and well, but we have hours of footage at VHS fast forward speed." I looked down at the time on my phone. "Does DoorDash come here? We're going to need sustenance."

TEN

I'd just polished off the rest of my chicken and mushroom tart when something on the tape caught my eye. We had to watch the entire day's worth of footage because I wanted to make sure nothing was missed. It ended up being a waste of time because absolutely nothing happened except us catching Lindsay on what appeared to be a heated phone call as she stood outside in the parking lot. A lot of wild gesticulating was about all I could see on the grainy footage, but it was enough to make me wonder what had happened before she came in.

The indoor footage caught Lindsay checking her cell phone over and over again until she pulled out a handkerchief from her purse and wiped her face. Nerves? Or fear? Regardless, she smoothed her hands down her outfit, squared her shoulders, and walked into the main area to teach her seminar. I saw the back of my head and noticed the moment I realized Lindsay wasn't there to teach. I sat up straighter and my shoulders stiffened before I got up a few minutes later and walked out. What I hadn't realized then was how long the evil look Lindsay had given me as I left lasted. A chill ran down my spine at her expression.

Moments later, the video shows Harriet and Lindsay in a heated discussion and Cole's arrival a few moments later.

"No sound?" I asked.

Harriet's sheepish smile told me what I needed to know. Great.

I watched as Lindsay snatched her purse out and stomped out of the store. Unfortunately, the camera views all required their own tape, so I had to switch the video to watch the rest of it. Cole followed her out, hot on her heels. They stopped by Lindsay's car, both of them gesturing wildly with their hands. I flinched when Lindsay's hand snaked out and slapped Cole in the face. He stilled. I had to imagine he'd been stunned. When she lifted her hand to slap him again, Cole showed great restraint. He caught her wrist, and with his other hand, opened her car door. He pointed at it and after a moment, she got in.

Cole shut the door and walked away. A great sigh of relief came from me, and I stopped the video and rested my head in my hands. "The police haven't asked for this?"

Harriet shook her head. "It's a small town. No one has cameras around here. I guess they assumed I didn't have any." She rolled her eyes. "That handsome one, I think his name was Cavanaugh, he said he might pop around today for more questions, though."

I blinked up at her. "Today?" I squeaked.

"Mmm hmm." She checked her delicate gold watch. "Around five, I think."

I looked at my phone and swallowed hard. 3:30. I still had time. Hardy would not be amused if he found me here scrolling through these tapes.

Harriet's eyebrows went up. "Problem?"

"Erm. Detective Cavanaugh and I are not on the same page..." My voice trailed off, and I gave her a sheepish smile.

Harriet laughed. "So. You are investigating, aren't you?" She leaned in and wiggled her eyebrows at me.

"I'm only trying to help a friend," I demurred.

"By investigating," Harriet deadpanned. She waved away my protests. "No matter. Let's get through the rest of this so we can see what happened."

I sped up the video for a few seconds. "Why didn't you think to look at these?"

Harriet sighed. "To tell you the truth, I forgot I even had surveillance. Hank comes in each night, switches the tapes out for me, and never says a word about it. I pay him in scones and three new releases each month. I've never had a problem with theft or anything else." She took the last bite of her salad and chewed thoughtfully. "If you hadn't asked me about it, I may never have thought of it. Hank does other things too. Maintenance mostly. The surveillance is just a task my father set him up doing, and I continued the arrangement." A fond smile crinkled the edges of her eyes. "He never complains or asks questions, just shows up, gets things done, and asks me if I need anything else. We grew up together, but I only see him if I work late."

From the wistfulness in her voice, it sounded like Harriet might be fonder of Hank than she let on. I pressed the button to stop the tape. Lindsay still sat in her car. Fortunately her windshield faced the camera, and I saw her pick up her phone and make a call. The video was too blurry to make out any of the words she was saying, but she stilled, and the phone slipped from her fingers. A person walked up to the car and opened the driver's side. Just as they reached in, the video turned to white snow on the screen.

I gasped. "Harriet?"

She looked just as stunned as I was. "Hold on," she cautioned, her voice trembling. She took the tape out, held it up to the light, frowned and put it back into the VCR. Harriet hit rewind, and we watched the last few seconds. My heart pounded as I hoped against hope it was a fluke. But... it wasn't.

Someone had deliberately either cut the cameras or deleted the tapes. It meant one of two things. Either they had someone else working for them or they had access to Harriet's shop. "Rewind it, please." My voice sounded hoarse with fear.

Logically, I knew I shouldn't be afraid of Harriet. She'd been a staple in this town for many years. Even my father had known her. But sitting here in this too small room, cooped up with someone whose evidence had just gone up in smoke, I couldn't help but feel a frisson of fear skitter down my spine.

I looked over at Harriet. The confusion and devastation on her face made my shoulders relax. "Do you think...?" I began.

She cut me off with a sharp gesture of her hand. "It isn't Hank." Her voice was firm, and the words were final. "There's no way he'd do something like this. And he wouldn't have a reason to anyway. They didn't know each other."

I didn't know how she'd know that considering she just admitted she rarely saw him anymore. "Mmm," I said more to myself than her.

Harriet snorted. "You think I'm an old fool." She shook her head. "No. Hank had nothing to do with this. I'd stake my business on it." She frowned at the snowy screen in front of us. "But someone had to have gained access to this room. This is where Hank stores all the tapes."

"Do you keep it locked?"

"Not always." One of her thin shoulders lifted in a shrug. "In fact, not nearly as much as I should. I've never had trouble with theft or anything here. We tend to trust people." Her voice trailed off not saying the words we both knew to be true.

Except when she shouldn't.

I gathered up my things and thanked Harriet for allowing me to go through the videos. Checking my watch, I let out a breath of relief. I still had thirty minutes before Detective Cavanaugh was due to be here. Just in case he decided to be early, I picked up the pace, cleaning up the remnants of my hastily eaten lunch and helping Harriet put the tapes back in order.

I couldn't tell whether the person in the video was a man or woman. They'd worn all dark clothing and had a slim build. It could go either way. What I hadn't wanted to admit to myself was the fact that the surveillance didn't clear Cole. In fact, it only served to add more questions. He very well could have left Lindsay, changed his clothing, and came back to harm her. Cole had a swimmer's build. He wasn't thin. Not exactly. But he had a slim-hipped grace to him.

As much as I didn't want to admit it, it was possible Cole committed the crime. Every instinct inside of me screamed he would never do something like this, but I had to put on my amateur detective hat and look at the evidence in an impartial way.

He had the time and the motive to do it.

It was now up to me to prove he didn't.

ELEVEN

The drive back to Silverwood Hollow was silent. I didn't bother to turn on the radio, content to stew in my morose thoughts. Cavanaugh was furious with me, and it would only get worse once he found out I'd viewed the surveillance before he had. Cole was being overly cryptic and wouldn't tell me anything.

Anger brewed deep inside of me at his behavior. He'd placed me in a terrible position and given me nothing to go on. I couldn't help the resentment I felt, almost like he'd played on my need to help people.

I picked up my cell and rang him. He answered on the second ring.

"Dakota, I asked you not to call me."

Annoyance made my nostrils flare. "Oh yeah?" I said,

seething with anger. "You expect me to risk my life for you and you won't even tell me what's going on!"

Silence fell over the line. When Cole spoke again, regret dripped from his words. "You're ... right." A whisper of something came over the phone. Cole rubbed his jaw when he was stressed. From the sound of it, he hadn't shaved in a few days. "I'm sorry, Dakota. I don't know what I was thinking."

Somewhat mollified, the anger within me snuffed like a candle. "I have to ask this."

He didn't wait for me to ask. "I didn't. I would never do something like that. Yes, I was angry. Yes, we fought. But I'm not a killer." His voice broke on the last word.

Silence fell between us. When he spoke again, he sounded defeated. "Come to my house."

I opened my mouth and shut it.

"I'll cook you dinner. And we'll talk. About everything."

"You cook?" I asked, stunned.

Cole's low chuckle rolled over the line. "I might be a bachelor, but I'm not helpless. I'm no gourmet cook, but I can make a mean chicken parm."

"Lucky for you, I love chicken parm. Can I bring anything?" The strange turn in this conversation left me a little befuddled.

"A bottle of red. How about 7:30 tonight?"

"I'll be there. I'll bring a salad, too." Hope lifted me and suddenly things didn't seem quite as dark as they had a moment ago.

"Vegetables, Dakota?" Cole griped, humor lacing his voice. "It's like you don't know me at all."

We hung up a moment later. A small smile tugged at my lips the entire way home.

COLE ACTUALLY *COULD* COOK. I hadn't known what to expect when I showed up five minutes early holding a bottle of Pinot Noir and a Caesar salad. He opened the door and the mouthwatering smells of red sauce and frying chicken wafted out to the porch. He'd put music on - Ella Fitzgerald from the sound of it. Suddenly my palms grew damp, and I took a mental inventory of what I had on and whether this could be construed as a date.

Why this just occurred to me as I stood on the porch of his house wearing slip on tennis shoes and capris that had seen better days, I had no idea. A lopsided smile hit my face as I shoved the bottle of wine at him. He frowned down at it, then looked up at me. I saw the moment he realized where my thoughts had led me.

Instead of reassuring me there was nothing even a hint romantic about this, he gave me a small smile, his eyes crinkling at the edges. "Really, Dakota? Would it really be so bad?"

Without waiting for me to answer - and I couldn't because even swallowing had become difficult - he stepped back from the door and gestured for me to come in. I stepped in and slid my shoes off, thankful I'd at least thought enough about my appearance to put on non-holy socks.

He led me over to the kitchen and opened the bottle. After he'd poured two glasses, he held his up. "To friends," he said, his eyes glittering with amusement.

Wordlessly, I clinked my glass to his and took a fortifying gulp of wine. I didn't miss Cole's grin as he turned back to the stove.

Get it together, Dakota, I admonished myself.

I refused to think this was a date. Doing so would make me too nervous to carry on a conversation and it was imperative we talk about everything going on.

Silence fell when Cole dished up two plates and set one in front of me. The aroma wafting from the plate made my stomach growl. Cole grinned at me as he sat down.

"I haven't eaten since this morning," I confessed.

"Word is you had a busy day," he quipped as he snapped his napkin out to lay on his lap.

This town... I sighed. If he heard I'd been at Harriet's, Cavanaugh knew as well. Maybe I would let his inevitable phone call roll over to voicemail.

Cole laughed out loud as he took in my crestfallen face. "You thought since you were in the town over word wouldn't get back?

That's exactly what I thought. I stuck my tongue out at him.

"Real mature," Cole said, but the grin he wore still hadn't fallen away. "Did you find anything out?"

His expression grew solemn as I laid out what I'd seen on the surveillance tape. Cole's jaw clenched once I'd fallen silent. "That doesn't look good for me," he noted.

I nodded. "Did you see anyone when you were walking away?"

He shook his head right away, dismissing my question.

"Think Cole," I urged. "Anyone in the parking lot? Even the smallest thing can matter."

He toyed with the rim of his wine glass and the space between his brow crinkled in thought. "A woman," he said a moment later. Cole squeezed his eyes shut. "Blonde hair, I think. She was too far away for me to tell how tall she was, but I remember she looked overdressed."

My thoughts went immediately to Sid and Chloe. "Two women from Lindsay's company were sent here after her death." I rattled off their names.

Cole grimaced. "I know them both, but it wasn't either of them."

"And how do you know them?" I picked up another piece of the chicken parmesan with my fork. If I was at home, I would have inhaled this and gone back for another slice. It was delicious.

"Through Lindsay. They came out with her a few months ago."

Interesting. They'd never mentioned that.

"And why was she here?"

Cole's eyes shuttered. "She was trying to open a spa here."

I waited. Cole finally sighed and closed his eyes. He rubbed his face and looked at me. "Someone in this town is embezzling city funds. I don't know who it is, but Lindsay mentioned some discrepancies when she tried to buy property here. The owner changed the price twice and said she hadn't paid some of the fees when she had." He shook his head. "It all looks really suspicious."

I sat up straighter. "Embezzlement?" That could definitely be motive for murder. I racked my brain as I tried to remember who worked in that department. I didn't get too involved with city business. For a long time, I'd kept my head down. Until Marcy. And now I wish I'd kept it down.

I bet Cole did, too, though it was a lot harder for him to stay out of people's business since his paycheck depended on it.

I gasped. "You're investigating it!" Stunned, I dropped my fork. "What are you thinking?!" The sharpness of my voice surprised even me.

Cole blinked, but his expression turned dark. "It's my job. You've known that since the second we met."

"This is Silverwood Hollow," I snapped. "You leave it to the police."

A bark of laughter escaped him. I knew how it sounded, but it was too late to take back. "I know," I admitted, throwing my hands up. "I know!" I dropped my head into my hands, aware of the appalling lack of manners as my elbows rested on the table. "This is different, though. I'm just a bookstore owner. If you make someone angry in the city, they could have your job."

"This is Silverwood," he agreed. "And corruption doesn't belong here."

"I don't understand what this has to do with Lindsay."

He picked up his wine glass and took a sip. "She was doing some digging for me." Grief passed on his face. "She died because of me."

My mouth fell open. "Cole. No. She didn't. You aren't responsible for what happened to her."

"But I am. Once she started asking questions, it must have gotten back to the wrong people."

I reached over and touched his arm. "You aren't responsible for the actions of a depraved person. Don't blame yourself for this."

"I'm trying to be very careful to stay out of it. My boss has warned me off." He scrubbed a hand over his jaw. "Normally, we'd be like a bulldog if we heard something like this. It makes me wonder…"

"You think your boss is involved, too." It was a statement because I didn't think it needed to be a question. It was obvious what Cole thought. I thought the same thing. "Did he say why?"

He shrugged. "He said something about a lot of heat coming down on the newspaper. But that's never stopped us before. In fact, it made us even more dogged to get the scoop."

Cole tapped his fingers on the wooden table, his expression lost in thought. "It doesn't make any sense. Journalists all have one thing in common - a desire to get to the heart of the story. Liam is one of the best and he owns the building. I don't understand why he's backing away from it."

It didn't make sense to me either. I knew of Liam though I'd never had a conversation with him. He'd come into the store a few times to browse crime fiction. Other than a friendly hello, he didn't speak to me.

"Who do you think it could be?"

Cole shook his head. "A number of people. Liam might be involved. Maybe he's getting kickbacks to suppress the story." His eyes looked haunted over the possibility. "Things like this usually don't involve just one person. It's going to be several."

Everything made more sense now. "I don't understand what Chloe and Sid have to do with this."

"Maybe nothing," Cole admitted. "Maybe they are really here because the company sent them. She was getting kickbacks from the books, so maybe they're here trying to clean up her mess."

Maybe. But my intuition told me their presence signaled something deeper. And I was going to get to the bottom of it.

TWELVE

Poppy finally came home with me. The stubborn cat hadn't wanted to leave the store for days now, but today she let me pick her up and put her in the car with me.

As soon as I opened the door, she jumped out of my arms and went directly to the kitchen, staring up at me expectantly. Snorting, I went straight to the food container and dished her out some kibble. She sniffed at it and gave me a baleful look.

I regretted giving her part of my salmon a few weeks ago. Ever since then, Poppy had been insufferable. Considering I couldn't afford to eat salmon all the time, neither could my cat.

"Sorry, Poppy. You get what you get, and you don't throw a fit."

Poppy yowled. I chuckled and thought of Mom. She said that to me constantly which did a few things: made me happy with what I had (though that had taken way longer than Mom had probably wanted) and also created in me a bit of an entrepreneurial spirit. Granted, a bookstore wasn't a huge moneymaker, but I had what I needed and was comfortable. I just didn't eat expensive meals all the time.

After staring at me a few more seconds waiting for me to cave, Poppy threw her tail up in the air, swished it, and finally ate the food I'd given her.

"Grumpy cat," I muttered. I fished out my cell phone from my purse and scrolled through the messages, wincing when I found Harper had texted me three times.

I called her immediately. "I am so sorry," I said as soon as she answered.

"No worries!" Harper chirped, her voice full of her normal good cheer. "I just wanted to make sure you were okay. I got a little worried when I didn't hear from you."

I slumped against the wall. "Whatever would I do without you?" I said, more to myself than her. I didn't mean to take her for granted, but when I got caught up with something, I tended to forget about time.

"You can tell me if you're investigating that murder over at that other bookshop." Harper's tone was knowing, but there was a touch of censure in her words as if I'd hurt her feelings.

I had to get better about sharing. "Yes," I admitted. "Cole's wrapped up in this."

"Ah," she said. She grew quiet for a moment. "Just be careful. Do what you need to do. I have the shop under control. Plus, I could use some extra hours."

I straightened. Harper never asked for extra hours. "Everything okay?" I ventured, not wanting to get into her business but wondering if I could do something additional to help.

"I'm thinking about buying a house," she confessed.

A gasp escaped me. "That's wonderful!" Harper was young, around 25 if I remembered correctly. Still young enough to have a lot of freedom, but old enough to start shouldering additional responsibility if she wanted it. "Where at?"

"I'm not sure yet. I'm looking at Candlelight Springs, but I'd prefer to stay here if I can find a suitable house."

"Have you asked Jeff?" I broached the topic carefully. Jeff Bastian wasn't on my list of favorite people, but he had a soft spot for Harper. I thought maybe Harper had a soft spot for him, too.

"No." Her tone was short and clipped, cutting me off from wanting to ask further questions.

"Ahhhh," I said. "Everything okay?"

"Jeff is Jeff," she sighed. "Opportunistic down to the bones."

She wasn't wrong there. Jeff always looked for an in and always wanted to know how something could benefit him. Though, to give him the benefit of the doubt, he'd shown me a different side at the end of Marcy's case, and he seemed genuinely interested in Harper. I wanted to know what happened, but it wasn't any of my business. "If I can help in any way, please let me know. Even if it's schedule flexibility so you can view houses. We'll work it out."

"Thanks, Dakota. In the meantime, I'll man the shop. Be careful. Whatever is going on, it isn't worth you getting hurt over."

I wanted to argue with that one. A good man might fall over this one, and I'd do whatever it took to ensure that didn't happen. "Thanks. I'll be in to open the shop in the morning, though." The doorbell rang just then. "I have to run. We'll chat more tomorrow."

We clicked off the line. Poppy ran to the door and sat like a sphinx, staring up at the door with an intense look that rattled me. I frowned down at her. She'd never done that before. I looked through the peephole and winced.

Hardy Cavanaugh stood outside my door, and he did not look happy.

I stared through the peephole as my mind raced for a solution. Escaping through the window came up in my top five just as Hardy knocked again. "I know you're in there, Dakota. I heard you on the phone. Open up, please, before I make this official."

I opened the door and blocked the entrance. "Detective Cavanaugh. How pleasant to see you again."

His eye twitched at my flippant greeting. "Cut it out. You know why I'm here."

Hardy's face looked like a storm cloud. Normally, his light blue eyes were calm and amused. Today they looked grayer, like summer thunderstorms. His mouth was pinched tight, and a frown appeared between his brows. I stifled the urge to smooth it out with my thumb.

"I do not know why you're here. Would you like to enlighten me?"

His jaw clenched. Guilt flooded me. I stepped away from the door. "Come in," I said, my voice resigned.

Hardy brushed past me, his body stiff with tension. He stood in the hallway as I shut the door. Suddenly I felt like my home had shrunk several hundred square feet. We stared at each other for a moment before I looked away.

"Are you hungry?" I asked. Poppy twined in between his feet. She loved Hardy.

Traitor.

He blinked as if surprised I offered. "I am," he admitted.

"Good." I pointed to the barstool at the kitchen bar. "Sit and I'll cook. We'll chat while I make dinner."

My thoughts strayed back to the dinner I had at Cole's place a few days ago. I hadn't spoken to him since that day, but we'd texted a few times. I'd taken today off from investigating and had meant to go into the store but realized I'd scheduled Harper for most of the week and the day got away from me.

Hardy appeared a little flustered. He sat down, a confused crease between his brows. Good. Maybe if I kept him off guard, he wouldn't yell at me.

Too much.

THIRTEEN

Hardy watched me like a hawk as I finely chopped shallots and added them to a sizzling pan of olive oil and a small pat of butter. This was one of my favorite meals, but it didn't save well and made too much. I felt wasteful every time I made it, so having Hardy here was somewhat of a blessing. I wouldn't feel guilty about wasting any of it with him here.

He hadn't spoken yet. Only watched me as I gathered the ingredients from the pantry and fridge. Chicken, shallots, mushrooms, bowtie pasta, fresh thyme I snipped from the window garden, bouillon, some other seasonings, and an expensive Balsamic vinegar I'd picked up from Jen's oil shop.

I broke the silence as I stirred the shallots. "Do you cook?"

"Not really. My schedule doesn't allow it." Hardy loosened his tie.

I pulled a bottle of red wine from the rack above the refrigerator and poured him a glass. I pushed it over without a word.

"My mom taught me how to cook, but it's not as fun cooking for one." He took the glass from me, and I studied his face. Lines of exhaustion etched the edges of his eyes and mouth. His eyes, normally so bright and blue, were darker and blue grey bags made his face look way more tired than it usually did.

Hardy grunted in agreement and watched as I browned mushrooms in the same pan as the shallots. The meal came together quickly and soon enough we were only waiting on the pasta to finish cooking.

When it finished, I sprinkled some fresh thyme on top of the sauce and gave Hardy a healthy portion of the dish with sliced chicken on top.

He accepted the plate. "We have to talk, Dakota."

I didn't answer until I'd made my plate. I sat beside him. "I know."

He dug into the pasta. I grinned as he closed his eyes for a moment. "This is delicious." He said it almost begrudgingly.

It was hard to stay mad at someone who'd just made you a home cooked meal. A secret my mother taught me long ago.

"Thank you."

We ate mostly in silence for a while. When Hardy was almost finished, he set his fork down with a sigh. "You visited Binders."

I nodded and kept eating.

"And you looked at the surveillance."

I nodded again.

Hardy snorted. "I was really angry at you when I got here."

"I know."

From the corner of my eye, I could see Hardy try to cover up a smile. "I find you exasperating, Dakota Adair."

"I know," I said again.

This time Hardy laughed to my surprise. "Tell me what you found," he said.

I blinked at him, and my eyes narrowed in suspicion.

He picked his fork back up. "I'm serious. It's obvious I can't keep you out of it, so tell me what you know."

"Will you tell me what you know?" I asked him.

"Nope." He gave me an infuriating grin.

"That seems awfully one sided."

"This is what keeps me from arresting you for interfering with a police investigation," Hardy said cheerfully.

I didn't know him well enough yet to know if he was joking, but from the way he looked on my doorstep, I didn't think it wise to push my luck. I took a sip of my wine.

"It makes Cole look bad," I admitted.

Hardy nodded. "Nothing in those tapes exonerates him. It only adds to the burden of guilt."

"He didn't do it," I insisted.

"I'm inclined to believe you." Hardy finished his meal and looked at the pan.

"Get as much as you want," I invited. "It doesn't make good leftovers."

Without being told twice, Hardy took the rest of the pasta and sauce and sat back down.

"If you trust me, I can help you," he said. "If you continue plowing blindly through murder investigations, you're going to get someone hurt. Or you're going to get hurt." His eyes darkened as he studied me. "I know Cole is your friend, but I have to ask you why he isn't the one out clearing his name." Hardy frowned. "Granted, I don't want any of you out there trying to solve a murder, but it's strange to me that Cole is relying on you for this." He didn't look happy about that at all.

I told Hardy the rest. When I finished, Hardy leaned back in the chair, a contemplative expression on his face. "It's always about money," he remarked, scorn dripping from his words. Finally, he shook his head and stood up, carrying his plate to the sink. I protested, but Hardy ignored me.

A minute later, he had a sink full of hot soapy water and he was washing my dishes. I blinked at the sight, uncomfortable at how homey and real it felt. My heart went lopsided and part of me wanted to run away. Instead, I wouldn't look a gift horse in the form of a handsome detective washing dishes in the mouth.

We fell into a silent rhythm; him washing and handing the dish over to me to rinse. I placed them all in the dish rack I kept on the side of the sink. Although I had a dishwasher, I rarely used it. Living alone meant I rarely made a big mess anymore.

When we finished and the dishes were all put away, Hardy leaned against the sink. He folded his arms over his chest and looked down at me. I felt tiny next to him, and it was like my house had shrunk several hundred feet. Hardy's presence was larger than life, but I didn't feel afraid.

I felt safe.

My internal alarm bells started ringing. Romance had been firmly off the table for a long time, and I had too much going on to start feeling all mushy toward someone I butted heads with all the time.

"I'm not going to stay out of this," I blurted. "Not until Cole's name is clear."

At the mention of Cole, Hardy's lips thinned. The moment was gone. "I'm well aware." He tossed the towel down on the side of the sink. "Thank you for dinner. I'll be on my way."

I wanted to say something to him. Ask him to stay. But I just didn't have it in me. I didn't know what this was, but I also wasn't sure I was ready to find out.

Hardy nodded and brushed past me. When he was gone, the house felt empty.

If I examined it close enough, maybe I did too.

FOURTEEN

I woke up the next morning and shoved any thoughts of Cole or Hardy right out of my head. I wasn't that kind of girl. I wanted the responsibility of a bookstore and a free life. Being tied down appealed about as much as a moth-eaten book. I didn't want to be lonely forever.

But I thought I might not mind being alone for now.

And I had a lot of other things to worry about.

Harper wasn't scheduled to come in until after ten this morning. I enjoyed the quiet of the dark store and as soon as I had everything ready to go, I walked down to Trudy's shop.

My steps slowed as I noticed a crowd of people gathered outside. Sprinkle Heaven was usually busy, but I'd never seen people out the door. Curious, I walked around and poked my head in the door.

"Dakota!" Trudy's voice called. I grimaced and gave an apologetic look to the line as she called me in.

Her red hair was wilder than usual, and she had a glow about her. "Did you hear?" she asked, her voice a little breathless.

I shook my head.

She grabbed my arm and led me to the front by the bakery display case. People milled all around and there was an air of excitement around the place. I nodded at several people I knew and locked eyes with a taller, thinner man wearing glasses.

Liam. Cole's boss at the paper. Bingo. I couldn't have asked for a better meeting. Meeting this way ensured I didn't have to follow him and like I didn't plan it.

His gaze skimmed away from me, but not before his jaw tightened. My reputation preceded me. I dragged my attention back to Trudy whose arms waved around with animation.

"And then he came up to me and asked me if I ever thought about opening another location!" Trudy put her hand over her heart. "A second location, Dakota. What a dream!"

"That's amazing, Trudy. Congratulations. What did it?"

Trudy grinned, her cheeks high with color. "That drink I came up with over the festival. I stuck it on the menu for a couple of days and he came in here and ordered one." She discreetly pointed at a man sitting at the back of the restaurant. "He's waiting for me to sign some paperwork."

The man was older, not traditionally handsome, but something about him made you want to keep looking. He wore glasses perched on the end of his nose. "He's legit?" I asked because I couldn't help myself. Stumbling into two murders in a short period of time made me suspicious of everyone.

She nodded. "I checked him out before I agreed to anything." Trudy leaned forward. "And that's not even the best part. We're having dinner once all the paperwork is signed."

I glanced back at him. "How old is he?"

Trudy laughed. "Old enough for me."

She had an ageless face but an adult daughter, so I placed her somewhere between her forties and fifties. "He's handsome," I noted as I nodded with approval. "Have a wonderful dinner."

She held up a finger and rushed to the back. I stood there feeling the weight of disapproving gazes on my back and waited. When Trudy came back out, she held a huge chocolate chip muffin and a to-go cup. "So you don't have to wait, honey."

I wrapped my hands around the cup and smelled. "Hot chocolate?"

"You know it." She jerked her head in Liam's direction. "I heard some rumors about that guy. You going to talk to him?"

My eyes widened. "Is that why you dragged me in?"

She grinned at me. "Maybe. Maybe not. It's better if I don't know, isn't it?" Trudy wiggled her fingers at me and went back around the register.

I shook my head in wonder and made a beeline over to Liam. He sat at a small table eating a scone and drinking a cup of black coffee. An open laptop sat in front of him, the light reflecting a sickly blue over his face. "Do you mind?" I asked as I pulled the chair out.

I bit down a smile as I could see his desire to tell me he did, in fact, mind, but he was too polite to tell me no. Few people would answer a question like that with a yes, and I banked on his manners to get my way. Dirty pool? Yep. But this was a murder investigation and if I had to be a trickster to get some answers, I'd do it. Reading all those detective novels over the years had probably given me a false assurance over my investigating skills, but sometimes faking it till you made it was the only way to plow through a problem.

He snapped the laptop shut, crossed his fingers together, and stared at me.

I smiled at him. "We haven't formally met." I stuck my hand out. A look of distaste rolled over his features so quickly I was sure I wouldn't have noticed it if I hadn't been looking directly at him. "I'm Dakota Adair. I run Tattered Pages, the bookstore a few doors over."

He knew all this. I'd seen him in my shop a few times, but I'd never taken the time to introduce myself.

He finally reached out and took my hand in a limp handshake. I stifled my shudder at the clamminess of his hands. Could he be nervous?

Liam's gaze flicked away toward the door, and I could sense his desire to extricate himself. I leaned forward. "I'm wondering if you're investigating a story," I began.

He held up a hand to stop me. "A good journalist wouldn't tell you what he or she is investigating." Liam sniffed. "Not if they want to keep their job."

I crossed my arms over my chest. "Alright then. What about if I gave you a tip?"

Annoyance rolled across his eyes. "And what tip would that be?"

"I have a few actually." I shrugged. "One is your employee, Cole. He's been released from jail, which I'm sure you know."

Liam's lips thinned. "I'm well aware of what's going on with my employees." His voice was like the Arctic.

"Then you know he was investigating corruption in City Hall?"

Liam blinked. His face went bone white. Silence ticked between us.

"I'm sure you know Silverwood Hollow has a proud history of being transparent in all their financial pursuits. Don't you think it's strange that Cole, someone who is dogged about every story, was suddenly arrested for a murder he didn't commit on the tail of him following some leads for this story?"

A muscle ticked in Liam's jaw. "I think any journalist who gets himself arrested for murder might not be a good journalist."

Shock stung me. "Really." I said, deadpan. "I'm pretty sure Cole has broken some of Silverwood's biggest stories including Marcy's murder just a few months ago. I can't imagine that a journalist who knows Cole well wouldn't smell something fishy about this." I leaned forward, crossing my fingers together in a mirror image of his. "And I find it very interesting that the word is Cole has been warned off the story."

Two spots of color appeared high on Liam's cheek. "You have no idea what you're talking about."

Realizing I might have gone too far with that last remark, I leaned back and out of his personal space. "Journalistic integrity and transparency have been Cole's life."

Liam sneered. "And what do you know about Cole?" he asked. "You've known him for what - a few months? And now you think you're an expert? I can assure you; you know as much as Cole wants you to know. Nothing more. Nothing less."

"How do you feel about stifling freedom of the press?" I asked, stung at his accusation. Yes, it was true I didn't know Cole as well as he knew me, but I thought maybe he was just a private person. Liam's words made me suspect something else was going on with him.

"There is no freedom of the press if I don't have a press!" he hissed. Liam shoved his laptop into a bag he'd slung over the edge of his chair. He left his coffee and scone on the table and snatched up his keys.

Seeing my chance of getting any information out of his evaporating in the wind, I threw out a desperate question. "Did you know Lindsay?"

He looked away but not before I saw something flash in his eyes.

Guilt.

"No," he snapped. "And if you ever approach me again, I'll have a restraining order slapped against you."

Liam marched out of the coffee shop, his laptop bag slung haphazardly over his shoulder. His steps were angry and people seeing his expression stepped out of his way.

"That went well," I muttered. I could just hear my mother now lecturing me about bees and honey.

I grabbed my purse and waved at Trudy on my way out, making sure I hadn't forgotten the goodies she'd given me.

A concerned frown wrinkled her brow, but she was too busy to come over. "Later," she mouthed.

Hopefully by later, this case would be solved and out of my hair.

FIFTEEN

My phone rang not five minutes later just as I stepped back into the shop. I grimaced as I looked down at the phone and saw who was calling. Guilt filled me as I hit the button.

"Dakota." Cole's voice was calm, controlled, and very, very angry.

"I'm sorry," I said meekly.

"I've been fired."

The cup fell from my hand, spilling sticky liquid all over the floor and the register. "Cole. I am so so sorry. I will fix this."

"Don't fix anything." His voice sounded weary. "Ever again. I'm sorry I asked you."

My stomach lurched and heat engulfed my face. "Don't say that. Please, Cole. I'll do whatever I can to get your job back."

"Do. Nothing. I'm completely serious. You've done nothing but make things for worse me since this started."

Hurt stung me right in the heart. "You asked me to help you!" I choked. "I can't help what's happened."

"You strong-armed my boss, accused him of having no ethics, and then tried to push him into a confession!"

"I did no such thing," I said hotly.

I could almost see Cole pressing a finger into the space between his brows. "That's how Liam felt. And I could see how he felt that way. So he acted accordingly to rid himself of the problem."

"I'm the problem!" I shouted. "Not you!"

"Yes, Dakota. That's the truth." The line beeped leaving me standing there in stunned silence.

I WENT through the motions of running the store, completely numb. I'd lost one of my very best friends due to my actions, and that friend had lost his livelihood. Could I have screwed this up any worse if I'd tried?

The bell rang and Harper breezed in, her hair in a long pony-tail. She wore little makeup, a pair of skinny jeans and a long t-shirt top with a pair of wrap around sandals. Over the t-shirt, she wore a long navy-blue cardigan and a long silver necklace. She looked hip, well rested, and ready for a day's work.

I felt like I'd been hit by a truck and could sleep for a week.

She smiled at me, but it slowly slid off her face as she took in my expression.

"What happened?" she demanded.

I shook my head and pointed over to the romance section. "*Not now*," I mouthed. I wouldn't say anything that could get back to anyone else. I'd already messed things up for Cole. I didn't want to make it worse. Though I wasn't sure how I could.

I'm sure I could find a way if I tried hard enough, though.

Harper's brows drew together, but she nodded. As she brushed past me, she gently squeezed my shoulder. "It will be alright," she whispered.

I nodded, but the sick feeling wouldn't leave me. I didn't think it would be alright ever again.

WHEN THE LAST customer had left for the day, I slumped back into the rolling chair at the register and groaned. A large delivery had come in after lunch and I stared balefully at the boxes wishing I didn't have to unpack them. Harper flopped down in the seat next to me and stared at them too.

"Is there a reason that's such a huge order?" she asked. Harper sounded amused by it. I frowned and rubbed my forehead.

"Christmas." I shrugged. "We're already late setting everything up."

"Do you think you can move all that product?" She sounded doubtful.

I nodded. "It isn't all books, though. I bought some decorations as well." We'd done the book tree which added a very cool spark of style to the store, but my window still looked like a pale reflection of the holidays compared to everyone else's stores around Silverwood.

Harper groaned and stood up, stretching her arms. "Why don't you go on home? I'll start tackling this."

I started to protest, but Harper gave me a look. "Seriously. I don't mind. You look like you've had a tough day."

I had to assume Cole's day was much worse than mine. "I'm giving you a raise," I announced suddenly.

Harper froze, then blinked at me. "Seriously?"

I stood. "Yes. Effective immediately. And paying you overtime if you stay and take care of these boxes."

Tears swam in Harper's eyes. "Thank you, Dakota. That's very generous."

I shrugged. "It's the least I can do for leaving you in the shop constantly while I run around and mess everything up."

Harper's mouth turned down. "We both know that isn't true."

"I got Cole fired today."

Harper sat back down in her chair, stunned. "Well," she said after a moment. "Maybe it's true today."

A surprised laugh bubbled out of me. Harper snorted and moments later, we were both laughing so hard we were breathless. I wiped tears out of my eyes and noticed a little while later that my stomach was no longer tied up in knots.

Harper reached over and slung an arm across my shoulders. "If there's one thing I know about you, I know you'll fix this. And you'll find out who's responsible for Lindsay's death. Try not to be so hard on yourself. It will work out the way it's supposed to."

I nodded, but I still felt terrible over what happened with Liam and how it affected Cole. "I just hope I don't lose him as a friend."

She shook her head. "I don't think you will. But I do think maybe you should look a little closer at Liam. Firing Cole seems like a knee-jerk reaction at first, but maybe it was the perfect excuse to get rid of him so he can keep getting away with something." Harper shrugged a thin shoulder and got back up.

As she bent down to start opening the boxes, I thought about her words and realized she was right. A second later, I grabbed my purse. "Thanks, Harper! I'm going to head out. Call me if you have any problems."

She waved a hand at me but didn't say anything.

"Poppy!" I called. "You coming?"

I headed to the back to look for the grumpy Persian and found her licking her paw as she sat under the table in the Young Adult section. "You coming?"

Poppy gave me an annoyed look and went back to grooming. "Suit yourself."

Before I left, I checked her food and water and told Harper the cat was staying.

"Cool. I'll invite her friends over and we can have a cat rager."

I snorted and left Harper and Poppy to their rager.

SIXTEEN

I pulled my hair up in an old ball cap I'd tossed in the back of my car and wore a large pair of sunglasses that obscured quite a bit of the top of my face. I didn't think he knew me well enough to know what kind of car I drove, but I'd parked down the block just in case.

Cole's former employer owned a building just outside of town. It was a nondescript place, brown brick, large windows, no landscaping—a gloomy place where people reported the stories around Silverwood and went home each night, only to get up and do it all again the next day. I hoped the inside of it looked better than the outside, because the front of the building looked soulless.

I checked my phone. Six o'clock. Everyone should be off soon. I tapped my fingers on the dashboard and turned on a podcast I'd been trying to get through for weeks now. Something about the history of Renaissance literature. I loved literature, but sometimes it was super boring.

As the host dragged on, I watched people begin to file out of the building. There was a woman who worked in the cubicle next to Cole. I met her at the Harvest Festival last month. Some other people I didn't know waved to each other, but there was no Liam.

Once the last car had left the parking lot, I pulled up a little closer to the building but realized I couldn't see in at all. All the blinds had been drawn up tight. Frowning, I inched a little closer and stopped before I ended up right in front of it.

I looked around to see if there were people milling about outside and when I couldn't see anyone, I slid out of the car, tugging the baseball cap lower on my face. I shoved my hands in the pocket of my down jacket and hurried over to the left side of the building, looking around to see if anyone was watching.

THE BACK of the building was just as soulless as the front, but this time it had only a couple of windows. The blinds were slightly open, so I hovered at the edge of one of them and peeked in.

A break room. I chewed my lip in frustration, checked the other window, then crept to the other side, fully cognizant that I looked like I was about to rob the place.

The right side of the building had one window cracked slightly open. I crouched down and peeked inside only to realize I had a perfect view of Liam. I reared back for a moment while my breathing calmed down and peeked back in.

He sat at his computer, his tie and hair askew. A thunderous frown sat on his face, and I watched as he pulled a bottle of brown liquid out of his desk and poured a glass.

Whiskey or something similar. I frowned and kept watching. The phone rang and he snatched it up. "Gazette," he barked.

I watched as his posture changed. He sat up straighter and looked around furtively. I drew back from the window until I could barely see him.

"I told you not to call me here," he hissed.

I leaned in slightly to better hear him. I wished at that moment I had supersonic hearing so I could understand what the person on the other end of the line was saying.

"That's not important. That meddling woman is getting into our business, and I had to fire one of my best reporters today! This is not what you said would happen."

He listened for a few seconds and snorted in derision. "It isn't worth it. I can't believe I got tangled up with you."

He paled as the person on the other end of the line said something.

"You and I are done. Our arrangement is off. I never want to hear from you again."

Liam hung up and dropped his head into his hands. A long groan came from his throat and when he straightened, he gulped the glass of liquid straight down.

I sat there for another couple of minutes before I crept away.

Liam was somehow tangled up in this. I just needed to figure out how.

BACK IN MY CAR, I rummaged through my purse for some lip balm when my fingers brushed against a folded piece of paper. I frowned and unfolded it just as I remembered what it was.

The note Poppy had showed me.

2409 Silverwood Maple Lane. I started up the car and headed to the address unsure what I would find.

THE STREET WAS LINED with gorgeous silver maple trees and dappled shade dropped the temperature by close to ten degrees. I shivered as I pulled my jacket closer and stepped out of the car. I checked the note again and looked around at the houses. Most of them were built in the Craftsman style with cute wrap around porches and brightly colored doors. The one I needed looked a little different. It was also in the Craftsman style, but the paint had been neglected and peeled from the side of the house. As I walked across the street, I noticed the stairs were beginning to warp. The silence in the air unnerved me a little. No cars or music or anything lent the street a frozen in time air. I stepped onto the first step gingerly and winced as it groaned beneath me. I hurried onto the porch and peeked into the windows but couldn't see much through the film of age and dirt.

I knocked on the door, but it opened underneath my knuckles. I froze in alarm. This was starting to feel like every horror movie I'd ever watched. I pushed the door open slowly, stiff with fear. It groaned underneath the weight of my hand.

I stepped in and immediately reared back. Something smelled in here. Dust, mold, disuse, and possibly something more sinister. I covered my mouth with the sleeve of my jacket and walked into the home.

Why in the world would Lindsay have wanted to meet someone here of all places? The place looked like it should be condemned.

But just as that thought crossed my mind, I looked to the left and stopped. The room next to me had been redone from floor to ceiling. The floors gleamed with brand new dark hardwood flooring. Deep maroon paint darkened the back wall and black and white printed wallpaper was used as an accent for the side wall. A strange looking bed sat in the middle of the room. It almost looked like one of those beds you saw in a doctor's office that you had to awkwardly sit on during an examination, but as I stepped in and saw the thicker mattress, I realized what I was looking at.

The beginning of Lindsay's spa.

I put my hand over my heart as tears pricked the back of my eyes. I couldn't condone how she'd done it, but to see someone's dream ripped away so harshly made my stomach sink. I left the room alone and wandered through the rest of the house.

Two more rooms were close to completion—one of them a deep blue with white and silver accent wallpaper and a wall full of nail polishes and a massage chair with a pedi-cure sink in front of it. The other was a room covered from baseboard to ceiling in Himalayan Salt. I gasped as I walked in, marveling at the creativity of the room.

I knew a little about the properties of the special pink salt and goggled a bit at how much this must have cost her. A large, comfortable chair sat at the back of the room next to a table full of magazines. A dehumidifier sat unplugged in the middle of the room. Shaking my head at the waste of it all, I backed out of the room and walked into the kitchen.

Where I found Sid's body.

SEVENTEEN

A strangled scream escaped my throat as I stared down at the prone body of the unpleasant woman who'd come into my bookshop only a few days ago. My back hit the wall and my hand crept up to my heart which beat like a frightened rabbit.

I dug through my purse, scattering pens and coins all over, as I searched for my cell phone. A fleeting thought about Hardy came and went, and all I could think about was getting out of the house and away from Sid's lifeless body.

"911, what's your emergency?"

"This is Dakota Adair." I rattled off the address. "There's a body. Please hurry."

"Ma'am, are you sure this person is deceased?"

From the way her eyes stared upward looking at nothing, I was sure. "She's dead," I confirmed. "Please send the police." I hung up before I thought better of it and took a step toward Sid.

She wore another pair of slacks, this time red, and a black, long-sleeved sweater. On her feet were black kitten heeled boots. A small pool of blood had formed around the back of her head. I dared not get any closer. Screwing up a crime scene would make this entire thing worse.

I turned and fled outside.

LESS THAN A MINUTE LATER, my cell phone rang. I answered without looking and before I could say hello, Hardy spoke.

"Are you safe?"

Tears pricked my eyes. "Yes," I whispered. "I think."

Road noise came through the phone. "I'm on my way. Where are you?"

"Sitting in my car outside the house."

"Are your doors locked?"

I nodded then realized he couldn't hear me. "Yes."

"Good." Hardy hung up, and I rested my head on the steering wheel and gulped in deep breaths.

He hadn't yelled at me.

But I knew it was coming.

I HEARD the police sirens before I saw the cruisers. Moments later, I was surrounded by law enforcement and paramedics. It seemed a little excessive since I knew the woman inside wouldn't need medical assistance.

More important than those people was Hardy. He walked toward me, dressed in slacks and a pullover sweater, his expression carefully blank. I slid out of the car and shoved my hands in my pockets because I didn't want him to see me fidget.

"Are you okay?" he said as he stopped in front of me, just inside my personal space.

I nodded.

"Dare I ask why you're here?"

I met his eyes. "I'm sure you already know the answer."

He sighed. "I checked this place out just the other day. The victim must have come here last night."

"Sid," I said and cleared my throat. "Her name is Sid. Was Sid." I looked over at the house. "This is the place Lindsay was turning into a spa."

"Looks that way." Hardy took out his notebook. "Tell me what happened from the moment you got here." He clicked his pen. "And then I'll take you for coffee, okay?"

"Okay. There isn't much to tell." I went through what happened as soon as I got to the house, leaving off me following Liam. When I finished, Hardy closed his notepad.

"Anything else you need to tell me?"

I'd tell him some of it. "I got Cole fired."

His eyebrows shot up. "Do tell," he drawled as he leaned against my car, his eyes sparking with interest.

I told him what happened with Liam at Trudy's shop and watched as he winced in sympathy. "I can only assume he's pretty angry at you right now."

I nodded miserably. "I think I lost my friend."

He shook his head. "Don't panic now. Let's see how this all comes out in the wash."

"Stained," I blurted. "Tide won't get this out."

Hardy chuckled. "Yes, but you always seem to come out of things okay."

I wasn't so sure this would be one of those things. "Let's hope," I said.

Hardy straightened. "Stick around for a while, okay?" He looked back at the house. "I'll be in there for a while, but when I get back out, why don't we get a coffee?"

I tilted my head and studied him. "Sure," I said after a moment. This was new. And he still hadn't yelled at me. Had the world tilted on its axis or something?

"Good." He jogged across the street, looking back at me once. Moments later, he disappeared into the house.

"Huh," I said to myself. Shrugging, I crossed the street and sat down in the grass to wait for him. It was cold, but I needed the fresh air.

ABOUT HALF AN HOUR LATER, Hardy poked his head out of the door. "Dakota?"

I blinked in surprise.

"Yes?"

"Can you come in?"

I stood and wiped off the seat of my pants. Surprised at his request, I didn't say anything for a second. "For what?" I couldn't help the suspicion in my voice.

Hardy's eyes crinkled at the edges. "We found something that might fall more into your expertise area than ours."

Intrigued, I carefully picked my way over the steps. He handed me a pair of shoe covers, gloves, and a mask. Once I put them all on, Hardy motioned for me to enter.

The mask helped a little with the odd smell in the house, but Hardy passed me over a small tub of something.

"Rub this inside your mask. It helps."

I opened it and a strong smell of menthol wafted from the container. I put a couple of dabs on the mask and my eyes started watering immediately. Hardy's lips quirked up. "It's better than the alternative."

I handed the tub back and let him lead me through the house. We took a detour to avoid the kitchen and walked to the back toward a room I hadn't seen yet.

When Hardy pushed open the door and I saw the inside, I stopped dead in my tracks.

"My God," I whispered. Books. Everywhere. Floor to ceiling books. Some were in boxes, some crammed on the bookshelves lining all the walls. Others were in haphazard piles on the floor. Some were even stacked on the windowsill. I cringed as I wondered how long those had been there. Fortunately, there were curtains on the window, so most of the books hadn't been exposed to as much light as those had.

"Can you take a look and see if any of them hold value?" Hardy rubbed the back of his neck. "I'm no expert, but just at a glance, I think she has at least a couple hundred thousand in books here."

My head jerked up at that. "What?" I didn't wait for his response. I stepped into the room and pushed a stack of paperbacks out of the way. I got down onto my knees and gently began sorting through the books, Hardy an afterthought in my mind.

I barely heard the door close behind me.

TWO HOURS LATER, I had a crick in my neck and a sore back. I'd taken books worth very little and sorted them into piles. Then I'd separated the books I couldn't believe she had into different piles and put them in the closet so they wouldn't be exposed to the light. Hardy didn't tell me I couldn't, and I wasn't sure how long the books would stay here, so I did what I would have done if I didn't have the right materials to pack them.

A soft knock on the door sounded a moment later. I stood, wincing in pain, just as Hardy came through the door. "We've been finished for a while. How's it going in here?"

I leaned against the wall, resisting the urge to sneeze. "I don't know where Lindsay got some of these books." Shaking my head, I looked up at the ceiling, fighting back tears. It felt silly to get so worked up over books, but Lindsay had books in here I'd never even seen before, much less handled.

"There's over five million dollars in rare books here, Hardy."

Hardy's eyes widened comically. "No," he breathed.

"Oh yes," I said. "And you're lucky I have some moral fiber, because this would set me up straight into retirement if I got my hands on some of these."

Hardy smiled at that. I'd never be able to afford any of the books in here. "There's a first edition English language Bible over there." I pointed over to the right wall where the closet door stood open. "It's worth about three quarters of a million."

Hardy whistled low under his breath. "Then there's a first edition of Dickens' Christmas Carol. Probably worth about half a mil." I looked around the room. "I've never seen anything like it."

"Do you think they're stolen?"

An exhausted laugh pulled from me. "If not stolen, probably not obtained honorably considering Lindsay was running a scam with rare books. Maybe she extorted them." I shrugged. "No way to tell."

Hardy walked over and peered down at the expensive Bible. "Three quarters of a mil? That's insane."

"That's books." I slipped the sweaty gloves off my hands and shoved them in my pocket. "I won't touch anything. I promise." My eyes skated over the books one more time. "What's going to happen to them?"

Hardy sighed. "No idea. The property belongs to Lindsay, and we found the books here. We'll see if she has any next of kin. If not, I'm not sure."

"Any chance of these being auctioned off?" I asked hopefully. Whether or not I'd be able to afford them was an entirely different story. Maybe someone who didn't know what they were doing would sell them off. A girl could dream.

"You'll be the first to know," Hardy said as he held the door open for me. "Still up for that coffee?"

I pulled my cell phone out and glanced at the time. "As long as it's decaf."

"Deal," he said.

EIGHTEEN

I followed Hardy to a coffee shop in Candlelight Springs, but just as I was about to turn off my car, my cell phone rang.

"Everything okay?" I asked Hardy, finding it odd that he called me when I was right next to him.

"Raincheck?" he asked. "I just got a call I have to go to. I'm so sorry."

"No worries," I said as I tried to tone down my disappointment. "It's been a long day anyway. I should check in on the shop and head home."

"Alright then. Be careful."

I smiled. "Always."

Hardy snorted before he hung up.

I watched him pull away and decided to grab a cup of coffee anyway. *Beans and Brew* was the local shop here, though I had to guess they couldn't compete with Trudy's creations. When I walked in, though, I had to reexamine that thought. The smell of freshly roasted beans hit me, and I inhaled, feeling my shoulders finally fall into a normal position. I hadn't realized how tense I was until I'd finally gotten out of that house. Fortunately, I was able to forget about the body only a few feet away from me once I became immersed in the books. This was the first time since I found her that I'd been able to really examine what had just happened.

Sid wasn't a nice person. If she was, I'd never seen it. She seemed rude and condescending both to me and to Chloe. I could only assume she knew more about Lindsay's death than she'd let on. Or she had something to do with it. I was leaning heavily toward the theory that Sid might have been the killer, but finding her body threw a definite wrench into that line of thought.

It wasn't out of the realm of possibility that she could have participated in it, though her being the killer was no longer viable.

I stepped up to the register and ordered a dirty chai latte, deciding at the last minute to go with black tea. It had caffeine but not as much as regular coffee, so it should be okay.

Just as I sat down to wait, the conversation behind me caught my attention.

I was in a booth and my back was to them, but I could tell it was a man and a woman.

"My business has been suffering for years," the woman lamented. "The last thing I needed was something like that to happen in my shop."

I stilled and strained to listen.

Harriet. The owner of Binders was right behind me.

A low male voice spoke. "I know things look bad now but give it time. Soon enough there will be something else to talk about."

Harriet sighed. "I don't know, Hank. Maybe I should give it up."

A sharp intake of breath sounded. "Harriet," Hank snapped. "I never want to hear you say that again. Binders is your dream."

I heard a shuffle and a softer sigh. "I'm so glad you were able to break away. I feel like we haven't seen each other in ages."

"All you had to do was ask. I would have come."

The barista waved at me. I whispered a silent prayer she hadn't called out my name. Tugging my jacket closer around me, I was careful not to let Harriet see my face.

"Thank you," I murmured as I took the latte from her. I ducked my head and took a sip from the drink as I rushed outside.

BACK IN MY CAR, I sat there wondering about what I just heard. Harriet didn't sound like she was involved in Lindsay's death, but what about Hank? I didn't know him, but it seemed like he really cared about Harriet. What motive could he have had to do it, though? If anything, it would complicate Harriet's life. If he cared about her, he would avoid doing anything to damage the business.

Wouldn't he?

I groaned and pulled out of the parking lot, my head spinning with the possibilities.

I CALLED Harper on the way back and she threatened me with bodily harm if I stopped by the shop. Though I wanted to see the progress on the store, I knew Harper could be trusted, so I headed straight home. Never in a million years did I think I'd be on a murder scene for half the day. All I could think about was putting my feet up and having a nice glass of wine.

NINETEEN

My phone rang around seven that evening.

"Hello?"

Harper was on the end of the line. "I'm so sorry to bother you, but Poppy is yowling up a storm. I tried to get her and take her home, but she refuses to come with me. When I tried to leave, she kept winding in and out of my feet trying to trip me!"

I snorted. "I'm so sorry. I'll pop by and grab her." Tattered Pages wasn't too far away, but I'd already changed into pajamas. I put a cardigan over my tank top and added a jacket over that before I grabbed my car keys.

Harper looked ragged when I opened the door. Her eyes were thankful as she quickly hugged me. "I'm so sorry. I'm supposed to meet friends at eight, but I didn't feel comfortable leaving her in this state."

"It's okay. Next time you can leave. Don't worry about her. She'll be fine."

Harper nodded as she sailed through the door. "Good luck!" she called.

Poppy sat on her haunches staring up at me, her wide green yellow eyes staring at me with a disturbing intensity.

I put my hands on my hips. "Well. What is it?"

Poppy stood and leapt up to the register. She put one paw on the phone and looked up at me.

"I'm not having more salmon delivered, cat."

Poppy yowled at me and pawed the phone again. Sighing, I walked over to it only to see the message light rapidly blinking. I looked at the cat. Poppy sat down staring at me with that same strange intensity.

This cat was seriously weird.

"Fine," I sighed as I picked up the receiver. "I hope I won the lottery."

I went through three messages about picking up orders and was about to get annoyed with my cat when a woman's voice came on the line.

"You have to help me," she whispered. "Sid is dead. I don't know where else to go. I'm afraid they're coming after me next."

Chloe. I straightened and scrambled through the register drawer for a pen. She rattled off the number and an address, but I listened to the message twice before I hung up. Poppy licked her paw and looked very satisfied with herself.

Just what kind of cat had I gotten myself saddled with anyway? I shook my head. "You want to come home?"

Poppy stared at me for a moment before she hopped down and wandered to the back. I followed her just to make sure Harper had filled her bowl up. When I saw Poppy eating, I reached down and scratched the back of her ears. "You're a strange cat," I murmured.

Poppy ignored me.

I decided I didn't have time to go back home for regular clothes. I dialed Chloe's number on the way to the address I'd scrawled down.

"Hello?" Her voice was quiet and withdrawn.

"This is Dakota Adair."

"Dakota!" Her voice was way too relieved to be talking to a bookshop owner.

"Why didn't you call the police?" I asked.

"I don't know who to trust. Lindsay -" her voice choked. "She had so much money tied up in everything. She knows everyone. I don't know who's involved or whether they're working for someone who is." She sniffed. "Can you just come so we can talk about this in private? I know it seems paranoid, but two of my coworkers have died and I'm afraid I'll be next."

"I'm on my way." I took a turn on a street I'd never been on before. It straddled the border between Candlelight Springs and Silverwood Hollow. A buffet restaurant with bright lights sat on the corner along with a small bed-and-breakfast and a row of two-story houses. "Are you at the bed-and-breakfast?"

"No. The house with the red door next to it."

"I'll be there in a minute," I said and clicked off.

Something about this didn't sit right with me. Chloe acted clueless every time I'd spoken to her. So why did she now know more? Or had she known something was wrong all along? I let my gaze skim the area. Seeing nothing out of place, I got out of my car, careful to take my phone out of my purse and put it into the pocket of my leggings. The long cardigan hid the bulk of the phone.

Just in case.

I knocked on the door and Chloe answered right away. She grabbed me by the arm and pulled me into the house, looking left and right as if we were in a spy movie. She closed and locked the door behind her and turned to face me.

"Oh, thank God, Dakota!" She flung herself into my arms.

Stunned, I could only stand there for a second as she wept into my shoulder. I patted her back awkwardly. "I'm not sure how I can help you, Chloe. I think you need to call the police."

Her normally perfect makeup had smeared under her eyes. Her hair was done up in a messy bun and she wore a tank top with a pair of workout leggings. Her feet were bare.

I followed her into the living room and saw a discarded tv dinner and an open bottle of wine. "Would you like a glass?" she asked me.

"No thanks." The rest of the home was clean, but I spied another empty bottle of wine in the kitchen.

"Listen. I have the number of a man you can trust. He's a detective, but he's actively working this case. I can assure you; he isn't corrupt."

"How do you know?" she asked me. Chloe chewed on her cuticles. She tucked the other hand in her lap, and I noticed the cuticles on her other hand looked red and angry.

"I can't know anything for sure," I told her. "But I'd trust him with my life." As I said those words, I realized how true they were. I didn't know if I believed Chloe's paranoia, but it was possible other people were involved.

Even Cole thought so. The thought of him sent a pang in my heart. I vowed to make things right between us.

"I won't call him," Chloe said. "I want you to help me. Sid knew you were involved in this somehow. Then she overheard some people talking about some other woman. Mary, I think her name was."

I sighed. "Marcy. I'm not an investigator."

"But you're good at it," she insisted. "At least that's what those other people said. I need help. I think I know who did it."

My eyes widened. "Oh?"

She nodded and looked around furtively. "There's a man who works in that bookshop in Candlelight Springs. Sid says she saw him in town the day before Lindsay died. She said he had a dirty shovel in the back of his truck."

"Maybe he did his landscaping?" I asked.

She shook her head. "That's what I said, but Sid insisted something was off about him. When he went into the hardware store, she peeked inside his truck. He had rope and a copy of Wuthering Heights. Sid said it looked old."

Wuthering Heights was an odd choice for an older man to read. It still didn't make him a murderer. "And what else?"

She blinked. "What else what?"

"What other evidence do you have besides that? Everything you told me is circumstantial. The police won't touch it. A lot of people around here have rope and shovels. A lot of people read." I tilted my head. "I should know. Most of them frequent my shop."

Chloe frowned at me. "Sid said she found out Hank was pining for that bookstore owner Lindsay hated so much. Harriet, I think her name was."

I already suspected that.

"But even more than that, Sid said she talked to someone who saw Hank in the parking lot right before they found Lindsay's body!"

"You should have led with that, Chloe."

She blinked at me. "Oh." She pointed at the wine. "Sorry."

"Did she say who she talked to in the parking lot?"

Chloe shook her head. "I don't think so. She just mentioned it was a woman."

"I think it's Hank." She sounded so sure, but I thought there were a lot of leaks that needed to be plugged before I put his name in the hat of suspects. It was odd that he was in the parking lot around the time of Lindsay's murder, especially since Harriet said he only came in the evening, but there could be a lot of other explanations. I didn't recall seeing Hank on the surveillance, but I stopped looking at the tapes soon after the murder.

It also didn't make sense on Harriet's side. Anyone would know a crime like that would bring a terrible spotlight down on a business. I'd have to think about this more once I extricated myself from Chloe.

"I still think you should call the police," I said as I stood.

She reached out and took my arm. "No. Not until we're a hundred percent sure."

"We aren't law enforcement." I extricated myself from her. "Stay inside and keep the doors locked. I'll try to see if I can find out more about Hank."

"I'm really scared, Dakota." Chloe's eyes were red rimmed from crying.

Sympathy outweighed my annoyance. "I know. I'm not sure what's going on here, but I promise I'll do my best to figure it out." I reached over and put my hand on her shoulder. "It's going to be okay. Just keep your head down and lie low. This is a small town. Who knows you're here?"

She chewed on her lip. "Just the owner of the house."

"Who's the owner?"

"A woman named Lauren."

I blinked. Where had I heard that name before? "Do you know her last name?"

"No. She seems nice. She's young, too."

"Tell no one else you're here. I have to get back home because I have an early day tomorrow. I'll call you when I have more news."

"Okay." Chloe watched me until I left the house. My shoulder blades itched as I felt her eyes on me.

Something didn't sit right about this. I didn't know what it was, but I planned to get to the bottom of it.

TWENTY

The next morning, I sat in the parking lot of Binders waiting for Harriet to open the doors. At 8:55 sharp, an old blue car pulled into the parking lot and Harriet stepped out. Her face was drawn with exhaustion, but her hair was done up perfectly. She didn't see me as she walked in which was weird because I was the only other person in the parking lot. Harriet was lost in her thoughts.

At nine, she opened the doors. I waved at her as I got out of the car. Surprised, she waved back and held open the door as I jogged over.

"Dakota. I'm surprised to see you. What can I help you with?"

I smiled at her. "I have a few more questions if you don't mind."

"Sure. Come on in. You want a cup of coffee?"

"I'd love one." I followed her back to the office and Harriet filled up a Styrofoam cup and handed it to me.

"There's creamer and sugar over by the cart next to the mini fridge. Help yourself."

I doctored my coffee and let Harriet settle in. When she took her first sip of coffee, I perched on the stool by the desk. "I'm sorry I have to ask this," I began.

Harriet squeezed her eyes shut. "It's about Hank, isn't it?"

"It is."

She sighed and set her mug down. "I promise you it wasn't him."

Surprised, I halted in the middle of a sip. "How do you know?"

A faint blush covered Harriet's cheeks. "Because he was in my office waiting for me during Lindsay's presentation and afterward. He only went into the parking lot after the police say she died." Harriet's lower lip trembled. "He didn't have time, but even if he had, he wouldn't have. Hank is a wonderful, kind man."

"And your boyfriend?" I ventured.

She nodded miserably. "I just wanted something on my own for a while without all the gossip hounds in these two towns trying to ruin it for us."

I knew how she felt. "Did you tell the police?"

"They didn't ask about him. I didn't feel the need to tell them."

A sigh escaped me. "Okay. I believe you. But you might have to talk to the police about this if word gets back to them about Hank."

"I know. Dakota, I don't know who did this. I can't help but think they were targeting my shop, but I don't know for sure."

"I think it's a lot more complicated than that," I assured her.

"Isn't it always?"

I smiled at her and stood. "Thank you for the coffee. I know you must be very busy, so I'll leave you alone."

Harriet stood and walked me out. "Please call me the moment you know something new."

"I will."

BACK IN THE CAR, I realized that everything I found out had done me little to no good. All roads led back to Cole. Maybe Liam as well, but he didn't seem guilty either. I decided to try one more thing before I turned everything I knew over to the police.

City Hall here I come.

· · ·

THE SILVERWOOD HOLLOW City Hall building was a pretty gray brick structure three streets over from my shop. I looked down at myself, frowning at my choice of attire today. It would have to do. I wore leggings, calf-high waterproof boots, a white t-shirt, and a long brown cardigan. I'd done my hair up in a large bun and wore dangle earrings. Casual, but hopefully not too casual for City Hall.

A man exiting held the door open for me. I thanked him and walked in, surprised at how festive the interior was. I really needed to finish decorating the store or the town would think I was a Scrooge.

I had no idea what I was going to do, but I made my way over to one of the windows. City Hall and the Tax Office were combined. I suspected it might be the tax office I needed because the issue was about property taxes. Maybe.

But just as I was about to step up and speak to the woman behind the window, a familiar gravelly voice spoke.

"Dakota Adair! Is that you, darling?"

I froze. I knew that voice. I also knew it meant trouble. I turned. "Hi, Aunt Corky."

She peered at me through thick Coke-bottle glasses. For years, she'd been blind and flat out refused the help of any form of glasses. Mom told me recently they'd tried to take her driver's license away, and she threw such a fit about it, she'd caved about the spectacles. Her watery blue eyes were still sharp as ever and I squirmed as she studied me.

"Come over here and give me a hug," she said.

I snorted and walked over. She pulled me closer and whispered in my ear. "I hear you're doing a lot of digging these days. Tell me what you're here for and I'll help."

Having Aunt Corky help with anything was a scary proposition indeed, but when she pulled back and I saw the look in her eyes, I knew I didn't have much choice.

"I'm trying to figure out who runs the property tax division, but I'm also trying to see who owns a certain property. Actually, two properties."

Aunt Corky's eyes narrowed. "Property records are public info, so you can pull those up with a quick Googler search."

"*Google*," I corrected.

"*Google*, Gaggle," she said and waved a hand. "Whatever that fancy search thing is. I know who runs the property division, but I wonder if you have specific questions to ask?"

I didn't. Not anything that wouldn't get me kicked out of the building. "I don't. I'm just following up on something."

"Hmph." She pulled me by the arm. "Come on."

Just then my grandma walked into the building. I wasn't sure how this day had skidded off the rails so far but having my grandmother and Corky in the same room was a disaster waiting to happen. If you put the two of them together, they looked about the same age, but I knew Gran was in her 80s. Corky was somewhere in her sixties. Mom would never tell me, and Corky always told everyone she was still in her forties. From her steel grey hair and her white tennis shoes, everyone who met her knew that was a lie.

"Mom!" Corky called and waved.

Gran's face lit up at the sight of us. She beelined toward us. "What are you two doing here? Getting into trouble I hope!"

I stifled my sigh. "Hi Gran."

She pulled me into a floral scented hug. "Hey honey. Where's your mom?"

"No idea. Probably at yoga." Mom tended to avoid my shenanigans. Just like I wished I could.

Gran snorted. "She never did win that French teacher over." She rolled her eyes. "But she keeps going back to try. I swear. I think she likes the class now but refuses to admit it because she's stubborn as an old swan."

I had to agree with my gran. Mom *was* stubborn. For months now she'd been complaining about the new French yoga teacher. The last I heard from Mom; the woman was still insufferably rude.

"Dakota is here to find out some property info." Corky leaned in close. "For the murder," she whispered too loud.

Gran's eyes lit up. "Murder you say! Some of the ladies from my Bridge group saw you leaving Cole's house the other night. Are you finally going to give us some grandbabies?"

"Gran. No." She wasn't nearly as bad as my mother, but she still hinted around every once in a while. Gran chuckled. "Oh relax. All in good time. I'm still hoping for Hardy. He still in the picture?"

"No one is in the picture. Can we please just get the info so I can get out of here?"

Corky clucked her tongue. "Now Dakota. Is that any way to treat your elders?"

It wasn't. "Sorry," I muttered.

Gran linked her arm through mine. "Let's go get you the info you need, honey. Then I'm sure we'll both be famished, and we can go to lunch."

My Gran. That's how she got you.

We opened the door to the tax office. A little old lady sat at the desk squinting at us through larger glasses than my Aunt Corky had on.

"Tilda!" Corky exclaimed. "How are you, you old geezer?"

I choked on a laugh and quickly turned it into a cough.

"Is she drunk?" I whispered to Gran.

"Not even a tipple, honey. You obviously haven't spent enough time with her."

Tilda cackled. "Just as well as you are, you old arthritic cow."

Both ladies laughed their heads off leaving me and Gran to watch the show.

"I'm here with my niece, Dakota. Come here, honey," Corky gestured to me. "Let Miss Tilda see your teeth."

"My teeth are fine." And seriously. What was up with people wanting to see my teeth? Like a broodmare going to auction or something.

"Honey," Tilda said, "your teeth are the window to your health! And they tell me the future."

"The future?" I echoed.

"Oh yes. I can tell how many children you're going to have and when you're going to get married. Now lean in and grimace, darling."

I shot an alarmed look at Gran, who shrugged. Then I looked at Corky.

"Well go on then. We don't have all day!"

I leaned in and grimaced. If it got me the info I needed, I'd do whatever she asked.

"My!" Tilda said. "You're going to have a gaggle full of children!"

I did not want to know the numerical equivalent of a gaggle.

"And you're going to marry a handsome man. Maybe three years? Four if you don't act right."

A surprised bark of laughter burst from Gran.

"Thanks for the tip, Miss Tilda," I said and closed my mouth.

"Any time, honey. Now, what can I do for you?"

I WALKED out of there with a strong appreciation for the strength of the Silverwood Silverette gossip chain. Not only did I have the name of the person who ran the office, I had the property records dating back ten years for the two houses I'd asked for. Then she told me she'd seen Cole and Lindsay getting mighty close two towns over a week before she died. That tidbit left an uncomfortable feeling in my stomach, but I squashed it down. Cole was a grown man, and he could do whatever he wanted.

It was obvious to me now. Cole and Lindsay had *definitely* been an item, no matter how he defined it. They say people are usually murdered by those closest to them, but I still wouldn't believe my friend would do such a thing.

I was missing something. A vital piece of this puzzle.

GRAN, Corky, and I went to lunch at a small little cafe named Springer's. The weather was too cold to sit outside, so we chose a booth toward the back. Just as we'd placed our drink order, Corky elbowed me hard in the side.

"That's him. Mark Palmer. He's the guy who runs the property tax division." Corky glared at him. "I heard he runs around on his wife, too."

Gran shook her head. "That's unproven, Corky. You know the Silverette Code. One of us has to witness it before it becomes truth."

My eyebrows rose. The Silverettes had a code?

"Look at the man," Corky grumbled. "Can't you see how he's looking around? He's on the prowl for a new young thing to spoil." Corky paused and gave me a hard look. "That's how you get him!" she announced suddenly.

Gran's eyes widened. "Corky."

"Bait!" she cackled with delight. "I bet you can get that man to tell you anything if you toss that dark hair and those pretty blue eyes at him."

The thought of it left a bad taste in my mouth, but I could see her point.

"Dakota," Gran warned me. "Be careful. Corky doesn't always give out the best advice."

Corky rolled her eyes. "You and I both know that's the fastest way to his heart. Besides breaking straight through his chest."

"Aunt Corky," I admonished.

She snorted. "With a hammer."

I scooted out of the booth and headed over to Mark. He was tall, a little overweight, and had a handsome face with a receding hairline on top. I stepped up beside him. "Hi," I said.

His eyes flicked to me and away but went right back to me when he realized I probably met the young enough demographic he required. Though I wasn't a spring chicken anymore, I still looked younger than my thirty-three years.

"What's good here?" I asked.

"Anything. I eat here once a week. My favorite is the pesto, but you won't go wrong with anything." He leaned closer and lowered his voice. "Except for the muffins. I'm not sure where she sources them from, but sometimes they're stale."

I gave him a brilliant smile. "Good to know."

He held out his hand. "Mark."

I shook it, trying to stifle a shudder at how clammy his hand was. "Dakota."

His eyes gleamed. "Dakota. You run the bookshop, don't you?"

"Guilty. Tattered Pages is the name."

"So, you're a big reader?"

"Definitely. I sell new, used, and rare books." His expression flickered at the mention of the rare books. Interesting. "We get in all kinds of cool texts." I flashed a rueful smile and saw Corky give me a thumbs up. "I wish I could keep all of them, but a girl has to make a living!"

"Rare books? What's the coolest one you've ever seen? I'm a big reader too."

I thought about the books I'd seen at Lindsay's house and took a chance. "I just recently came across a first edition of The Bible translated into English." I couldn't help the envy in my tone even as I baited him. "It was an incredible book and worth a bundle." I shrugged. "Alas," I said dramatically. "It wasn't mine."

"Was it at a store?" He stared at me intently.

"No. I can't remember where I saw it. Private collection, I think." There was no way I was telling him what house I found the book at.

"I would have loved to see it."

I bet he would have. "What do you do?"

He held up a finger and rattled off his order to the young woman who came over to the register. "I work at City Hall in the property records division. Boring stuff."

"Not boring at all!" I assured him. "I've heard Silverwood Hollow is an up-and-coming town. It's about time. I think we've been sleepy for way too long!"

He smiled at that. "I heard there was a spa supposed to be opening soon."

My heart lurched, but I wouldn't let myself get too excited. He worked in the property area, so it wasn't out of the ordinary that he knew this. "Oh really?" I hope he couldn't tell my interest was feigned. "Who's opening it and where? That's so exciting. We've never had a spa here."

He leaned a little closer. "I think ownership switched hands just recently."

I hadn't had the opportunity to open the envelope Tilda gave me yet, but I *definitely* found it interesting about the property changing hands. Lindsay hadn't even been buried yet. "Really? I wonder why. Doesn't that usually mean there's a problem?"

A condescending smile flickered over his lips. "Not at all. Just an issue with the paperwork."

The woman handed him his tray of food, but before he took it, Mark handed me a business card. "What do you say to dinner? My treat. We can chat some more. I'd love to hear more about these books."

"And I'd love to hear more about this spa!" We laughed as I took the card. I wished him well and watched him walk over to a small table at the front of the restaurant.

I LET OUT A DEEP, relieved sigh. The young woman behind the counter studied me for a moment before she dropped her voice. "Be careful. He's creepy. I saw him with that woman who died a few days ago. He looked really angry at her."

I blinked. You never knew where the best information would come from. "Really?"

She nodded. "The poor woman looked absolutely ragged and you could tell that guy wanted to yell at her. He took her by the wrist, and it looked like he was holding her too tightly."

I glanced back over at Mark who was staring at me. "Thank you..." I looked at her name tag. "Marsha. I really appreciate it."

"Any time!" she beamed at me. "What would you like to order?"

TWENTY-ONE

Gran, Corky, and I went our separate ways. I drove straight to the bookstore to relieve Harper. When I pulled up in front of Tattered Pages, my breath left my body.

The window display was something out of a Dickens' novel. Harper had set up fake snow and a village display complete with ceramic cars, houses, people, street signs. Anything a small village would have, she had put in there. The entire thing was lit up and fairy lights rested in the snow.

I slowly got out of the car, unable to take my eyes off it. When I opened the door, I stopped at the entrance. While the book tree was still the main attraction, Harper had strung lights all around the shelving and set up a cozy Christmas village scene right as you walked in. Soft instrumental holiday music streamed through the speakers. I looked down when I heard a soft bell and Poppy sat at my feet staring up at me accusingly. Harper had replaced her collar with a red and green one, complete with a jingle bell.

"Well, aren't you the cutest thing I've ever seen," I murmured.

Poppy hissed at me, turned, and stuck her tail straight up in the air as she walked away.

Harper laughed. "What do you think?"

I turned to look at my assistant. "I think I'd be feeling really guilty right now if I hadn't just given you a raise!"

Harper blushed, a pretty wash of color on her cheeks. "Thank you. I thought I'd help you out. I know you've been really busy lately."

"With everything except the store," I said ruefully. "This is incredible, Harper. Why don't you take off early? I'll pay you for the full day."

Harper clapped her hands together. "Seriously?"

I nodded. "Of course. You outdid yourself today. Thank you."

Harper smiled at me and took off her name badge. Before I could say much else, she'd snatched up her purse and rushed out of the store.

Well. Apparently, she had somewhere to be.

I grinned and stuck my purse behind the counter. Two people browsed through the nonfiction section, but other than that the store was quiet.

I put the envelope on the counter and grabbed a notepad from the drawer. It was time to figure this murder out.

Once and for all.

TWENTY-TWO

I jotted down what I knew in a linear timeline starting with what I remembered about how many times Cole had been seen with Lindsay before her death.

Then I jotted down the info the barista had given me about Mark while I was in the coffee shop. Both of them had been seen with her just before her attack, but when I asked Liam if he knew her, he didn't answer but looked guilty.

If I crossed Cole off completely, it would leave a few people. Hank, who Harriet insisted wasn't guilty. Mark, who was certainly creepy but it didn't mean he was a murderer. Then Liam. I knew he'd gotten himself tangled up in this somehow, but since I didn't know who was on the other end of the line, I didn't know how or with who.

Lindsay had taken over the rare books business from her family and from what Chloe and Sid said, she hadn't wanted to do it but thought she could make some quick cash scamming people.

But then why did she have a stash of millions worth of books in her closet?

Was this about the books or was this about the spa? Not much led me back to the books other than her scamming people to make the money to open her spa. Somehow the city of Silverwood Hollow had gotten tangled up in this, too. Or maybe Lindsay tangled herself up in it.

Cole hadn't been re-arrested. A hopeful sign. Maybe Hardy was focusing his attention elsewhere.

If only I could get him to compare notes with me. I chuckled under my breath at that one. Fat chance.

I took a break to ring up a few customers, but when the lull in business came, I tackled my notes again.

I jotted down Sid and Chloe's names and mulled them over. Sid seemed to know way more about Lindsay's dealings than Chloe did, but when Chloe had called me, she seemed to know way more than before.

Had Sid told her? Or was she somehow involved?

I tapped my pencil on the notepad and sighed. I was missing something, but I couldn't figure out what.

Shuffling my paper, I pulled out the manila envelope Tilda had given me. I shook out the contents and spread the papers around me. Just then, my watch alarm went off and I realized it was closing time. No one else was in the store, so I left the paperwork there and went to lock the front door.

Just as I reached up to turn the lock, I noticed Chloe standing outside. She waved at me and jogged up the steps. I held the door open for her and let her in.

"What are you doing out?"

She hugged her arms over her chest. "I needed to see you. Something has happened."

"And you couldn't call?" I asked. "I'm closed now. Can it wait?"

Poppy came out just then and rubbed up against my ankles. She sat after a second and stared up at Chloe, an intense look in her yellow green eyes.

"It can't wait." She rummaged in her purse and pulled out a piece of paper. "Sid left this in her room. I just found it today. What do you think it means?"

Frowning, I took the slip of paper from her and opened it. At first, I didn't know what I was looking at. After a longer look, my eyebrows went up.

"Sid was involved in the book scam," I murmured. It made sense. Chloe and Sid had come on their company's behest. Maybe they were wrapped up in it too. "Did you know?"

Chloe shook her head, innocence in her eyes. "No idea. I don't know anything about books. I like romance," she confessed, as if it were something to be ashamed about. "I don't read anything historical or classics or anything like that."

"It doesn't matter *what* you read. It matters that you read," I said, my attention still focused on the note.

She had several books listed, most of them classics. I skimmed the last and found the translated version of The Bible, but it had been crossed off. I wonder what that meant.

"This one?" I pointed to it on the page. "Did she ever talk about it?"

Chloe peered down, one strand of blonde hair falling over her face. "Sid didn't really seem like a Bible kind of person. Have you ever come across a book like that?" She pointed to the number scrawled next to the name. "Is that how much it's worth?"

I nodded.

Chloe whistled. "It's odd that she kept saying there was no money in books, isn't it?"

I was starting to find this entire thing more than odd. "Do you know someone named Liam?"

Chloe blinked. "Can't say that I do." She shrugged. "Sid did most of the networking around here." A rueful smile crossed her lips. "I was always the sidekick." She hitched her purse up over her arm. "I just wanted to deliver that to you to see what you could make of it. I'm supposed to head home in a couple of days."

"Already?" I folded the paper and put it on the register.

Chloe's gaze flicked over to the manila envelope. "That from the property tax office?" Her gaze met mine.

Something flickered in her eyes. I nodded. "I had to run over there to get something for Mom."

"Oh, I thought it was for the case."

I didn't think she was close enough for her to see the writing on the pages, but suddenly I didn't want her to know what was on them. "No. Mom is thinking about buying a house and wanted to get the property values for the last few years."

Chloe's brow furrowed. "Can't you do that online?"

I shrugged. "You know how old people are." I held up my keys and made them jingle. "Really sorry, Chloe. I have to close up shop."

"Oh sure," she said, her gaze lingering on the folder. "I'll get out of your hair. It was nice to meet you, Dakota. Just in case I don't see you again."

"You too!" I walked her to the door and made sure it locked securely behind her.

I was unable to shake the feeling of foreboding that came over me for hours.

I MADE a pot of decaf and headed back over to my notes. The entire town square was shut down and the shop was quiet. Poppy had curled up next to me on top of the register, purring quietly in her sleep. I dared not touch her because she was being sweet.

I flicked on the desk light and studied the property documents, wondering why Chloe was so interested in them.

I skimmed down the first set of the house Chloe was staying at and saw the name Lauren. Why did that name sound so familiar? I racked my brain until I remembered the woman who'd come into the shop a while ago. The divorced one who'd bought the old Chambers' house. Odd she hadn't mentioned purchasing the other place too.

It didn't mean she was guilty, of course, and I didn't sense anything off about her, but I wrote her name down anyway.

When I examined the second set, my heart raced with anticipation. I'd never heard of the company before, but from the name of it, it seemed like books were somehow involved.

Emporium Antique Tomes. I slid my laptop over and Googled the name of the company. It took me about half an hour to discover who owned it. When the name popped up, a frown hit my brow. Rushing back to the office, I dug through the receipts from the last several days until I had what I was looking for.

I TUCKED all of my notes and evidence into the manila folder and folded it gently into my purse. I'd done my job. Cole wasn't guilty. I still hadn't connected all of the dots, but I'd connected the most important one.

Who'd killed Lindsay and Sid.

Just as I was walking out of Tattered Pages, a tall figure stopped at my door.

Liam.

Fear made my heart race. I took a step back.

He held up his hands. "I'm not here to hurt you. I'm here to help."

Wasn't that what all bad guys said? Right before they hurt you?

"Why did you fire Cole?" I demanded.

"To keep me safe." Cole came around the corner, his hands in his pockets, a rueful smile on his handsome face. The sun had set a while ago, but streaks of purple and orange still lit the sky. Their faces both stood in shadow.

I felt safe in this town, but I had two men who both had grudges against me. I couldn't help but feel a little nervous.

Cole must have sensed my discomfort. He laid a hand on Liam's arm and the man stepped back.

"From the look on your face, you know something."

"I'm not sure why you trust him," I blurted.

Liam had the grace to look sheepish. "It was a knee-jerk move, I admit. I got caught up in this and didn't mean to. I've been trying to break the city hall scandal for a while and the person feeding me info got cold feet."

"And wound up dead?" I ventured.

He nodded, grief flashing in his eyes. "Sid didn't deserve it. Neither did Lindsay."

The sound of a click from behind me stopped me cold. Cole's eyes widened with alarm. "Dakota!"

"None of you better move a muscle," said the voice. "Dakota, hand over the folder and your notes."

I slowly turned and extended the manila envelope over. "Not much of a reader, huh?"

Chloe smiled at me then, a hard look on her pretty face. "Just romance. The other stuff is way too boring." She chuckled. "But it pays oh so good."

It had taken me a while to discover who owned the Emporium company and, at first, the name hadn't made sense. It was only when I started digging into the public records and bumped Chloe's receipt up to the tax records that I realized she was using her maiden name. She held her left hand up and wiggled it. "Divorced two years now," she said. "He wasn't much of a reader either."

"Why Chloe?" Liam asked, his voice pained.

"How did you manage to buy the property out from under Lindsay?" I asked.

Chloe smiled then. "She ran out of money and needed investors. What she didn't realize was the gold mine she was sitting on. Lindsay couldn't tell a rare book if it bit her right in the nose."

That must have been why none of the books were stored properly.

"She inherited a company she had no idea how to run and then wouldn't sell it to my family." She shrugged. "She didn't realize we were the ones who invested in the property and leased it back to her."

Chloe waved the gun. "Now, you're going to tell me where her stash of books is. I know you know. I could tell when I talked to you."

"The police have those books," I answered honestly. "None of them were stored properly and some were damaged beyond recognition. You won't get nearly what they're worth." A lie, but she didn't know it.

Her upper lip curled in a snarl. "Where are they?"

"Why did you kill Sid?" I asked, hoping to draw this out until someone witnessed the standoff. From my peripheral, I saw Cole shift a tiny bit. I could only hope he was texting or making a call. Something to get us out of here.

"Sid knew too much. She discovered it had been me all along. Then she wanted a cut of it."

Liam inhaled a sharp breath. "She wouldn't."

"Oh, she did old man. As soon as she found out what those books were worth, she demanded a piece of the action. I tried to talk her into a cut of Lindsay's salon and we went over there to check out the progress." She rolled her eyes. "After all the excitement over it this town showed, I thought it had the potential to be a gold mine."

"But Sid threatened to go to the police," I said. It made sense.

"If I didn't give her fifty percent," Chloe said.

"So you killed both of these women. And what do you have to show for it?" Cole said.

I dared not let any expression on my face. Chloe had been in the house where those books were the entire time and hadn't figured it out!

She grinned then, just as a man walked out from the shadows. He wore a heavy jacket with a hood, but he was tall. When he came into the dim light of the street light, I sighed.

Mark.

Cole growled. "I knew it! I knew you were involved."

Mark spread his hands out. "Looks like the bookshop owner should take your job then. She's the only one who got close enough." He winked at me. "Nice try on the buttering me up tactic, though. If Chloe hadn't already stolen my heart, I would have bought you the lobster."

Um. Eww. I glared at him as the pieces slowly fell into place.

"This is the long game. You're manipulating property values and pocketing the proceeds! You priced Lindsay right out of her own property. She knew something was shady about that transaction."

Mark grinned. How someone could be so happy about someone killing two people as long as he got to keep pocketing money would forever elude me.

"It's a little more complicated than that, but you have the gist of it."

The records of this entire town would have to be audited once this was over. If we made it out alive.

"You tried to frame Hank," I accused. "How did you erase the video?"

Chloe rolled her eyes. "This is a small town and that old lady was tied up with Lindsay. It was easy enough to slip in and delete it." She snorted. "Although who uses VHS anymore? Seriously."

I couldn't wait to tell Harriet her new beau was off the hook.

"I guess you aren't going to let us walk away?"

Mark and Chloe laughed at that. "Not a chance." He tossed rope over to us. "Blondie, you tie your girlfriend up."

Beside me, Cole stiffened but caught the rope. "And then?"

He pulled out his own gun. "Then you two come with me. Chloe can deal with nosy over here."

The moment they separated us we were all dead. I glanced over at Cole and from the set of his jaw, he knew it too. He took both of my wrists and leaned over to tie me up. Chloe and Mark glanced away to speak amongst themselves.

"I'll keep this as loose as I can. You have to get away, Dakota. Promise me," he whispered urgently.

I nodded and he fastened the last of the knots.

When he stood, Mark gestured to Liam and Cole to go

ahead of him. "I have a van down the street. If one of you makes any sudden moves, I pull the trigger."

Moments later, I was alone with Chloe.

SHE TRIED to force me back into the bookstore. I didn't want to go back in there because it took me a long time to feel safe there again after what happened with Marcy. "Not the bookstore," I pleaded. "I don't want my assistant to find me."

Chloe snorted. "What do I care?"

"My cat is there, too."

Chloe gave me a long look. "So you don't want to traumatize your cat?"

I shrugged. "Mostly I don't want her to track blood all over the bookstore." That wasn't why at all. I didn't want to traumatize *anyone*, but Chloe seemed dark and maybe flippant answers were the way to her heart.

"Fine," she snapped. "I like cats, too, but they're bloodthirsty little things. I have a car one street over. Walk in front of me and say nothing if we pass anyone."

"I promise."

She motioned me with the gun and we headed the opposite way the men had gone. I walked right past Trudy's shop and noticed the lights on. I glanced into her store and we locked eyes. Her outdoor light was brighter than mine, something I'd change immediately if I made it out, and I prayed she could read my lips.

"*Duck*," I mouthed.

Trudy's eyes widened and she immediately dove beneath the display case. I breathed a silent sigh of relief when Chloe looked inside the shop. "Is someone there?" she demanded.

"No."

She pulled the door handle but thankfully it was locked. "You better be sure. I'll come back for her next."

"You put up a convincing innocent act," I said instead. "You had me fooled for quite a while."

"No one likes it when a pretty face has a brain."

I begged to differ. "Maybe you need better people in your life."

"Watch your mouth, Dakota. Or you'll wind up like Lindsay and Sid."

I really didn't think it would matter much, because I knew it would happen anyway. She was feeding me false hope.

CHLOE OPENED the car door and shoved me in. I thought about jumping out but I wouldn't have time before she saw me. I needed to wait until she relaxed her guard a little. Before the door opened, I started working at the knots Cole had tied, loosening them bit after bit until I had enough slack to get them off. Chloe pulled away from the curb and headed down the main street to wherever I was about to meet my demise.

At the first red light, Chloe stopped, looked around and pulled right through it. At that exact moment, an unmarked dark sedan turned on its lights.

I squeezed my eyes shut in gratitude even as I knew it wasn't over yet.

Chloe bit back a noise and met my gaze in the mirror. "You better not say a word, do you hear me?"

I nodded as she pulled over.

I couldn't see who got out of the car, but only a few people in this town had an unmarked sedan. Only one of them would know what was going on. I sent up a silent prayer even as my heart beat a thunderous roar in my chest.

HARDY TAPPED ON THE GLASS. Tears began to pour down my cheeks.

He didn't glance at me, though he had to know what was going on.

"Evening, ma'am," Hardy said, flashing his million dollar smile at Chloe.

She fluffed her hair and turned on the innocent act. "Good evening, sir! I am so sorry about that. I'm in a big hurry tonight. We're late for a party two towns over and I didn't see anyone coming." She giggled.

Hardy leaned against the car, a friendly smile on his face. His gaze flicked to me and back to Chloe before she even noticed.

"Well, we all make mistakes. I'll write you a warning, but first I need to see your license and registration."

"Oh," Chloe breathed, surprised. "Give me just a moment." She ducked her head to search through her purse.

Hardy locked eyes with me. "*Now,*" he mouthed.

I jumped out of the car and took off running. My heart pounded in my chest and blood roared in my ears as I ran. I dared not look back until I was safely inside of Hardy's car.

Sirens screamed around the corner and Hardy held his service weapon at Chloe's driver side window.

I let out a choked strangle of relief.

It was finally over.

EPILOGUE

Two gifts waited for me when I walked up to my porch a week after the Chloe debacle. One was in a pretty red gift bag and the other in a small elegantly wrapped box.

I took them both inside and tossed them on the table before I let Poppy down. She glanced up at me and dismissed me just as quickly.

I slid off my shoes and scooped both of the gifts up before I padded to my couch.

I opened the bag first. It was a handwritten thank you note and a bottle of good wine.

I owe you everything. I got my job back. And a raise.

It was signed by Cole.

Grinning, I put them back in the bag and looked at the box. There was a tag on it that only said: *For Dakota.*

I carefully unwrapped the box, feeling guilty at messing up the expensive wrapping paper.

Inside, I found a few things. A signed Christmas card from Hardy Cavanaugh. A set of handmade leather bookmarks depicting scenes from Lord of the Rings, a signed copy of Andy Weir's *The Martian,* which I hadn't had the chance to read yet, and two tickets to an Agatha Christie outdoor play about half an hour away. I opened the envelope with the tickets and saw a note written in his sprawling cursive.

You. Me. A fake murder. How about we solve it together this time?

A Shelf Indulgence Cozy Mystery Series

How about a ghost whisperer in a new magical town? Check out
The Psychic Cleaner series!

Psychic Cleaner

Like a little more magic with your cozies? Check out The
Magical Soapmaker Mysteries!

The Magical Soapmaker Mysteries

If you'd like a little more action and sass and don't mind some
PG-13 language, check out my Aphrodite series.

The Goddess Chronicles

Or, if you like a snarky bartender with a secretive mixed heritage,
meet Violet!

Cocktails in Hell

ACKNOWLEDGMENTS

If you want to keep up with my newest releases, please find me on the web at sebabin.com and sign up for my newsletters. I only send one out when I have a new release.

More wonderful things to come, and I hope you'll stick around to see them.